BITTER TRUTH

CJ LYONS

Also By CJ Lyons:

Lucy Guardino Thrillers:
SNAKE SKIN
BLOOD STAINED
KILL ZONE
AFTER SHOCK
HARD FALL
BAD BREAK
LAST LIGHT
DEVIL SMOKE
OPEN GRAVE
GONE DARK

Renegade Justice Thrillers featuring Morgan Ames:
FIGHT DIRTY
RAW EDGES
ANGELS WEEP
LOOK AWAY
TRIP WIRE

Hart and Drake Medical Suspense:
NERVES OF STEEL
SLEIGHT OF HAND
FACE TO FACE
EYE OF THE STORM

Shadow Ops Covert Thrillers:
CHASING SHADOWS
LOST IN SHADOWS
EDGE OF SHADOWS

Fatal Insomnia Medical Thrillers:
FAREWELL TO DREAMS
A RAGING DAWN
THE SLEEPLESS STARS

Caitlyn Tierney FBI Thrillers:
BLIND FAITH
BLACK SHEEP
HOLLOW BONES

PRAISE FOR NEW YORK TIMES AND USA TODAY BESTSELLER CJ LYONS:

"Everything a great thriller should be—action packed, authentic, and intense." ~#1 *New York Times* bestselling author Lee Child

"A compelling new voice in thriller writing...I love how the characters come alive on every page." ~*New York Times* bestselling author Jeffery Deaver

"Top Pick! A fascinating and intense thriller." ~ 4 1/2 stars, *RT Book Reviews*

"An intense, emotional thriller...(that) climbs to the edge of intensity." ~*National Examiner*

"A perfect blend of romance and suspense. My kind of read." ~*#1 New York Times* Bestselling author Sandra Brown

"Highly engaging characters, heart-stopping scenes...one great rollercoaster ride that will not be stopping anytime soon." ~Bookreporter.com

"Adrenalin pumping." ~*The Mystery Gazette*

"Riveting." ~*Publishers Weekly Beyond Her Book*

Lyons "is a master within the genre." ~*Pittsburgh Magazine*

"Will leave you breathless and begging for more." ~Romance Novel TV

"A great fast-paced read....Not to be missed." ~4 ½ Stars, Book Addict

"Breathtakingly fast-paced." ~*Publishers Weekly*

"Simply superb...riveting drama...a perfect ten." ~Romance Reviews Today

"Characters with beating hearts and three dimensions." ~*Newsday*

"A pulse-pounding adrenalin rush!" ~Lisa Gardner

"Packed with adrenalin." ~David Morrell

"...Harrowing, emotional, action-packed and brilliantly realized." ~Susan Wiggs

"Explodes on the page...I absolutely could not put it down." ~Romance Readers' Connection

This book is a work of fiction. Any references to historical events, real people, or real locales are used fictitiously. Other names, characters, places, and incidents are the product of the author's imagination, and any resemblance to actual events or locales or persons, living or dead, is entirely coincidental and not intended by the author.

Edgy Reads
Cover design: Toni McGee Causey, stock photo courtesy of Adobe Stock

Library of Congress Case # 1-6493536231

BITTER TRUTH

CJ LYONS

Chapter 1

THERE ARE SOME WHO SAY hunting animals for sport is cruel and barbaric. I agree. After all, animals cannot fully comprehend the fact that they are being hunted from afar, and when the knowledge of a threat finally emerges—if ever, given modern high-powered rifles and scopes—they react with thoughtless instinct. Where's the fun in that?

But humans... that's a different matter altogether. Stalking prey as cunning and dangerous as you are, who could easily turn into predator if given the chance... what greater challenge could there be?

I will never kill an animal for sport. But a

man? Why not? It's as much my life at risk as his; our commonplace, barbaric, primal fight for survival elevated to a game of wit and daring.

And if someone's too blind, too civilized, too soft, dimwitted, or slow to recognize me as a deadly threat when I have them in my sights, then they really are just dumb animals, deserving of whatever fate befalls them. Boring as chasing a rabbit into a snare. I prefer my game armed with wits, desperate enough to resort to teeth and claws, as capable of killing me as I am them.

It makes victory taste all the more sweet...

MAGRUDER COUNTY, IDAHO IS KNOWN for many things. The least miles of paved roads per capita. Not just in the state; in the entire US of A. The highest concentration of wolves, bighorn sheep, and mountain lions in the lower forty-eight. The lowest rate of violent crime in the tri-state area. The most arrests for poaching—although the citizens of Magruder County refuse to acknowledge hunting slightly out of season to put food on the table as a crime, the federal government that manages the three wilderness areas and two national forests that occupy most of the county still does.

The least accessible county seat in the state. The highest number of private airstrips—there being no paved roads beyond Poet Springs, the county seat. The lowest number of hospital beds, being zero since the nearest hospital is two hundred twelve miles away in Lewiston or east over the mountains to Missoula.

And the most flavorful huckleberries in the whole damn world. At least that was Sheriff Bill Beachey's opinion as he strode through a patch of fireweed, skirted a mound of bear scat that was at least a day old, and made his way to the clearing at the top of the cliff overlooking Blanco Canyon.

He snatched a handful of the tiny indigo berries and dribbled them into his mouth one at a time, savoring the moment when their skins burst open, releasing their flavorful juice. Huckleberries were even better when his wife, Deena, baked them into pies or the bread that she used to make French toast on Sunday mornings, or boiled them into jam she'd save for the winter months to remind them of these glorious summer days.

Winters were harsh here on the western slope of the Bitterroots, where arctic winds pounded their fists against unyielding granite peaks, howling, trapped in the mountains' embrace until the air shed tears of thick, wet snow that some days felt as if it would never stop. But when Deena brought out the huckleberry jam, one taste magically made summer seem not so far away.

It had been a hot July, and now, the first week of August, the berries were ripening quickly. He'd bring Deena here this weekend, Bill thought. Just like when they were first courting—and with Deena, unlike the girls who'd come before, it had definitely been courting, from the first moment he met her, forty-one years ago when they were both just high school kids. Pick some berries, then fall asleep with his head in her lap as she read aloud from whatever book she had handy, the summer breeze teasing her long, dark hair across his face, the last thing he'd see before he closed his eyes. Sheer heaven.

Couldn't have days like that back in Denver—not without his phone going off, interrupting them with a callout to a crime scene. After thirty years working the city streets, he'd thought he wanted to retire, come back home to these mountains, take up fishing or the like. But it turned out sitting around all day trying to learn how to relax was more stressful than working a triple homicide with the leads gone dry. He'd been slowly going crazy. Until Sheriff Langer had his heart attack—a mild one, a wake-up call, the doctors had told him—and asked Bill to fill in until the election.

Funny thing was, returning to law enforcement—even in a sleepy county like Magruder, where ninety percent of his time was spent in his Jeep, driving from one minor call to the next—had probably saved Bill's life. It had definitely saved his sanity and his marriage. He loved the job so much that last week he'd actually filed the paperwork to put his name on the ballot come November—the only name on the ballot so far, the county clerk who also functioned as their department's dispatcher and the county postmistress had told him.

The last drop of berry juice eased its way down his throat. Bill smiled and pushed the brim of his Bronco's ball cap up to better let the sun graze his face. He moved through the meadow to the edge of the cliff, facing east over the valley carved out by ancient glaciers and past it to rows of jagged white peaks towering over forests green with balsam, cedar, and pine, then beyond them to more peaks, these just across the state line in Montana.

He'd ask Deena to read him some poetry during their picnic, he decided. Yeats or Yates or some other dead Irishman. She'd love it.

He slid his phone from his shirt pocket and took a few photos for Deena. Loose pebbles cascaded down the sheer cliff face, bouncing off the boulders below. An innately cautious man—it was how he'd survived thirty years on the job in Denver—Bill stepped back.

Which was how he was caught off balance. A lightning strike of electricity surged through him, freezing his muscles, pain ripping down every nerve. Then a shove from behind pushed him over the cliff's edge.

At first he flew, his cry of surprise filling the air. Then he hit the rocky scree-covered slope and his howl was cut short. His body bounced and skidded against cruel blades of granite, not a tree or bush in sight for a handhold; the rocks offered no purchase, only more damage to his hurtling body. He flailed his arms up to protect his head but was held captive by gravity, and he hit the ridge with a sickening crack of bone that echoed across the gorge.

And then there was silence. As if the entire forest had paused, waiting to see if Bill were dead or alive.

For a long time, no sound came. Slowly, timidly, afraid to draw the attention of the predator on the cliff, the forest came alive once more. Then, amid the buzzing of insects and the rustling of leaves in the breeze and a variety of small animals intent on gathering food and the soft padding of carnivores stalking their prey came a foreign sound from the cliff's edge: human laughter.

Chapter 2

Lucy Guardino shivered as she sat in the air conditioning of the University of Pittsburgh's orthopedic surgeon's examination room. Given that most patients would be wearing thin hospital gowns or dressed like her in shorts and a T-shirt, the cold air seemed to serve to mainly add insult to the overall indignity of being a patient.

Waiting over an hour wasn't helping. Especially when she could hear Dr. Twame's deep bass laughter as he chatted with his nurses outside the room. Why was it that every orthopedic surgeon she'd encountered thought he was irresistible to women? And none of them seemed to know how to read a clock. She was always fifteen minutes early for every appointment; they were invariably at least an hour late.

At least this was hopefully her last appointment for a while. Even her physical therapist, a.k.a. the Sadist, said her recovery from the dog mauling that had almost cost her her leg had been remarkable. All she needed now from Twame was an answer for the new pain that was plaguing her: an almost constant tooth-rattling spike that radiated from mid-calf down to her little toe. She'd dealt with plenty of pain during her rehab—the lightning jolts of nerves healing; cramps and muscle spasms; a deep bone ache that drilled into her very marrow. She'd been able to grit through all of that and make it out the other side—until now, when she thought she was healed, that finally her life could return to normal, this new pain was threatening to slowly drive her insane.

"Lucy, Lucy, Lucy," Twame said as he pushed through the door, holding an X-ray of her ankle up before him as if it contained the secrets of the universe. "What am I going to do with you?"

He plopped down on the exam stool and wheeled it over to her. Even though she was sitting with her legs dangling over the end of the exam table, he was still tall enough to meet her gaze. Twame was in his mid-thirties with the build of a former football player—and the arrogance. "You know this is a masterpiece?" He waved the X-ray with its bristling hardware shining bright white against the grays and black of her bones and muscles. "You're my Mona Lisa. So why do you insist on ruining my handiwork?"

Given that it wasn't his ankle but hers—and that she had worked her butt off these past eight months, rehabbing it to be able to walk again, albeit with the help of a brace—she answered with a glare. "Bottom line."

His sigh ruffled the film he still held before him, preferring to stare into its depths rather than at his flesh and blood patient. "Most patients, this long out, I'd be discharging them from follow up, telling them to return as needed. But you..."

"Is it because of the times I re-injured it?" Nothing major. A pin twisted loose after she tackled a serial killer. A moderate sprain when she slipped and fell while outrunning a wild fire. Other injuries sustained after she'd left the FBI to join the Beacon Group as a private investigative consultant. Lucy's leaving the FBI hadn't exactly been voluntary—more like politically motivated. The powers that be under the new director had decided to retire her, citing a "career-ending" line of duty injury.

"Well," the surgeon hedged. "We always knew the damaged nerves would be problematic. Did the new meds help with the dysautonomia?" Fancy medical speak for the new pain with its almost constant electrical tingling that made her muscles quiver as if worms were crawling beneath her skin.

"No." Just like nothing else had helped. Not the TENS unit or the ultrasound or all the anti-inflammatories, anti-depressants, anti-everythings. She needed to be able to do her job without her injury putting anyone else at risk—a team was only as strong as its weakest link.

That night in January when the killer's dog had mauled her leg, it had robbed her of far more than skin and tendon and muscle and bone. The thought left her gripping the edge of the exam table—the sound of a the dog's rapid panting, the hot spray of its drool mixed with her blood, the smell of an animal surrendering to bloodlust overwhelming her. She blinked, fought for breath, and edged back to the present, holding the dog with its fetid breath and blood-smeared muzzle at bay. For now.

"The muscles are coming along nicely." They'd had to remove large chunks of muscle that had been crushed by the dog's jaws, and then go back and take more after she'd developed an infection. "Thank the PT for that."

The physical therapy that Lucy had relentlessly doubled up on, getting up before dawn to work out with Nick, her husband, and then going back on her own after work before going home.

"It's these bones," he continued. "There's

just only so much you can do with old bones. If you were a nineteen-year-old quarterback..."

"But I'm not." Her tone was sharp.

He lowered the X-ray but still didn't make eye contact, instead cupping Lucy's heel in one hand, scrutinizing the Gordian knot of scars stretching down her leg, crossing over her ankle before finally wrapping around her foot. "Have you given any thought to my alternative treatment option?"

Amputation. *Not* an option.

"It's easier to rehab after a BKA—below knee amputation—before you're forty. And the advances in prosthetics are amazing. I can guarantee virtually full function—more than what you have now—with a significant decrease in pain."

He finished his examination, dropped her leg, and moved to the desktop computer. "I think we need to seriously discuss it. One more injury, we might have no choice anyway. Better to do it on your terms, right?"

Typing a note, he signed his name with a flourish of his finger against the track pad and then clicked to the main page. "Oh. My mistake. You already are forty. Happy birthday." He glanced up. "Guess we should make this decision sooner rather than later." He consulted his phone. "I have an opening on the surgery schedule in three weeks. What do you say?"

Lucy grabbed her splint, a rigid piece of molded plastic that fit around the back of her leg and under her foot, and tightened its straps before putting her shoe back on. She leveraged her body down from the exam table. "I say I'm taking these old bones home. Maybe sign up for social security and assisted living on the way."

His deep chuckle rumbled around the room as he stood and held the door open for her. "This is why you're one of my favorite patients. Such a sense of humor. I'll pencil you in on the OR schedule; my nurse will call to confirm."

She walked past him, forcing her posture upright while hiding a wince of pain—in her haste, she'd pulled one of the straps on the splint too tight, and it was digging into a particularly sensitive area of scar tissue.

As she hobbled through the waiting area filled with teenagers and twenty-something athletes, he called after her.

"Happy birthday, Lucy!"

Chapter 3

As Lucy drove home, she decided to find herself another surgeon—one not as determined to slice and dice and discard vital parts of her anatomy. When she turned onto her street in Pittsburgh's West Homestead neighborhood, she rolled her shoulders, yawned to break the tension crackling along her jaw, and tried a smile.

Megan was visiting Nick's parents for the last two weeks of her summer school vacation, which meant no fuss over Lucy's birthday. A quiet dinner, followed by an early night enjoying the peace and quiet of a house absent a teenager: exactly what Lucy needed.

Then she saw a wheelchair-accessible van

that looked exactly like Wash's, her tech analyst from Beacon Falls. Weird. She passed the van and spotted black balloons flying from her mailbox.

The black banner across the garage door almost sent her driving around the block. *LORDY, LORDY, LOOK WHO'S FORTY.*

Oh, damn. Lucy stopped the Subaru just short of her driveway. Her phone rang; Nick. "What the hell?"

"Don't blame me. I know how much you hate birthday parties. And surprises."

And *most* especially surprise birthday parties. "Then who?"

"Megan. She arranged everything before she left—said you and I deserved a fun night out with grownup friends."

Lucy sighed, her fingers stroking the black paracord bracelet Megan had made for her last Christmas—and re-gifted her another on Mother's Day after Lucy lost the first one. Both she and Nick were introverts; she'd never understand how they'd conceived and raised such an extroverted daughter with her love of big, dramatic gestures.

Nick continued, "She didn't even tell me until she called today to make sure I'd be home before you. Half the neighborhood is here with their grills in our backyard. Plus your old team from the FBI, everyone from Beacon Falls—even Oshiro and June got a babysitter and made it."

Lucy turned into her driveway and somehow found the energy for a smile. "Maybe we should surprise her—they have a fairly decent high school down near your parents, right?"

"Are you kidding? A teenage girl living on a horse farm, no parental supervision, constantly being spoiled by her doting grandparents? She'd love it. We'd never hear from her again—at least not until she sent us the bill for college and/or her wedding."

"Yeah, you're right. Guess we broke her, we get to keep her." The thought of the planning that had gone into this and how Megan had kept it secret widened her smile. "She really did all this on her own?"

"Yep. Kid's some kind of logistic genius.

Even more of a genius convincing all the adults in on it to go along with their part of the plan."

Lucy opened the car door and swung her bad leg out first. There was no reason for it to hurt more than usual—other than the fact that the surgeon wanted to cut it off. But she couldn't think of that now. Now she needed to act surprised and excited to see a few dozen people tramping through her house and garden. "Okay, tell them I'm coming in."

"Love you, Lucy-loo." He hung up.

As Lucy trudged up her front walk, moving more slowly than usual to give Nick time to arrange the party-goers, she glanced at her phone and realized she'd missed several calls while she'd had it turned off at the doctor's. All from Bill Beachey, an old friend. She and Nick had first met him over a decade ago when he'd attended one of Lucy's classes at the National Police Academy in Quantico. Turned out Bill was a Civil War buff like Nick, who had grown up outside Manassas, so he and his wife, Deena, had returned to visit when they were on vacation the following year. They'd seen each other a half-dozen times since, visiting various battlegrounds together. Last year Bill had retired from the Denver force to return to his hometown in Idaho and then became the county sheriff a few months ago. The work was a lot easier, he'd joked when he called a few months ago to explain why they needed to cancel this year's trip—he and Nick had mapped out an itinerary of lesser known West Virginia battlegrounds—but Magruder County was broke, and with only two deputies to cover for him, Bill didn't feel he could take vacation so soon after coming on board.

Megan must have invited Bill and Deena to the party and he was following up, sending their regrets, Lucy thought. Before she could listen to his messages, the front door sprang open, accompanied by a chorus of "Surprise!" and she was swept into a maelstrom of music, laughter, black balloons and streamers, hugs, and well-wishes.

She dropped her phone onto its charger and didn't think about it again. Instead she surprised herself by relaxing and having fun, forgetting about her leg, her job, and her hatred of birthday parties. Even the dog, whose constant presence usually haunted her, was banished. Megan was right. She'd needed this—a night of fun with the people she loved most in the world.

It was almost midnight when the last guests finally left—after mostly taking care of the clean up, which was maybe the best birthday gift of all. Lucy hated housework and often neglected it to spend time in her garden. Luckily Nick was a bit of a neat freak.

As she and Nick were packaging and putting away the leftovers, her phone rang. Nick grabbed it from the charger. "Megan."

Lucy put it on speaker as she answered. "Hi, sweetie! What are you doing up so late?"

"Happy birthday!" Megan sang out, blissfully ignoring Lucy's question. "Were you surprised? Dad, was she surprised? For real, I mean, not just her 'I already figured it out but I'll play along anyway' fake surprise."

"I was really surprised," Lucy admitted.

"She was," Nick added. "But the black

balloons almost drove her off."

"Yeah, but I didn't want her soooo surprised that she wouldn't relax and enjoy the party."

Nick raised an eyebrow at Lucy, beaming at their daughter's advanced social psychology skills. Lucy smiled back. They really were lucky Megan only used her talents for good—she was far smarter than the two of them in many ways.

"It was a great party," Lucy assured Megan. "Thank you. Best birthday gift ever."

"Of course now you've raised the bar," Nick said. "Christmas, my birthday, our anniversary—"

"Don't forget Mother's Day and Father's Day," Lucy added. "Can't wait to see what you'll come up with for all those."

Megan's over-dramatic sigh echoed through the phone. "I've created a monster." She yawned. "Gotta go. I'll call you guys tomorrow, okay?"

"Love you, sweetie."

"Love you, too. Night." She hung up.

Lucy turned to Nick. "I know her being

gone is the closest thing you and I have had to a private vacation in years, but I miss her."

He leaned over to kiss her lightly. "She'll be back soon enough—but in the meantime, I have my own birthday gift to give you."

She kissed him back, draping one arm around his neck to pull him close. "I bet I can guess what it is."

He took her hand and they walked through the first floor, turning off the lights. As they crossed the dining room, heading toward the stairs, she remembered the missed messages from Bill Beachey. Nick went to lock the door and turn off the living room lights while she listened to Bill's voice mails.

"Lucy!" Bill sounded short of breath or excited. "I know this is going to sound weird, but I think I stumbled onto something here. Cold case, right up your alley. Call me when you get a sec. Thanks."

Another, time-stamped twenty-six minutes later. "I'd sure love to run some stuff past you. Call me any time, day or night."

Finally, an hour and forty-two minutes

after the second message. "Guess maybe I was wrong. But damn, I was certain. Anyway, if you have a few minutes, give me a call."

Nick returned as Lucy was staring at her phone, calculating the time difference, wondering if it was too late to call. "What is it?" he asked.

"Bill Beachey. He left three messages." That alone said a lot—Bill was one of the most laconic lawmen she'd ever known.

"Megan must have told them about your birthday. But wait, it was Bill, not Deena?" Deena was the one to make social calls; Bill only called to talk cases, Civil War history, or arrange the details of a visit.

"Actually he didn't even mention my birthday. A case—or something—he didn't leave any details. He sounded really anxious that I call him."

"They're three hours behind, so they'll probably still be up. Why don't you? Probably easier than catching him at work in the morning." Bill and his deputies were seldom in the sheriff's station; they spent most of their time on the road patrolling their expansive territory. Plus Magruder County was in a remote area of Idaho's Bitterroot mountains where cell reception was spotty at best.

Lucy dialed. No answer on Bill's cell. She didn't bother leaving a message; he'd know it was her calling back. Next she tried their residential landline.

"Hello?" It was Deena, but her voice was high-pitched and tight with tension.

"Deena? It's Lucy Guardino. Is Bill around? He asked me to call. Hope it's not too late; didn't wake you, did I?"

There was a long pause. "Lucy? You talked to Bill? When? Today?"

"He left me three voice mails earlier today. Late morning or early afternoon your time."

"What about? Did he say where he was? Or where he was going?" Deena's words skidded into each other as she rushed them all out in one breath.

"No. Deena, what's wrong? Did something happen?"

"I don't know. Lucy, he's gone. He never came home, and no one's heard from him. Bill's missing."

Chapter 4

"Book two tickets," Nick said as he hovered over Lucy's shoulder. She was sitting cross-legged on their bed, her laptop balanced on her knees. "I'm coming as well."

She glanced up at him, her expression hovering between *Hell, no* and *Thank God.*

"He's my friend, too," he reminded her. "I can help with the search, or help with Deena and the family..." He trailed off, not adding that his expertise as a trauma counselor would be most needed only if the worst had happened and Bill wasn't coming home again. He squeezed her shoulder. "He's smart, tough, and he knows those mountains. He'll be fine."

He was surprised when she didn't shrug

away his false hope. Instead, she covered his hand with hers. "I hope so."

They booked the first flights available—it turned out getting from Pittsburgh to a town that literally sat at the end of the road surrounded by three sprawling national wilderness areas was more difficult than it appeared from a glance at a map. The fastest route took them from Pittsburgh to Atlanta then to Salt Lake City before finally landing in Lewiston, Idaho, still over two hundred miles to their final destination of Poet Springs, the Magruder county seat. It meant ten hours of air travel followed by a long drive, and with the time difference, they would arrive mid-afternoon. Nick hoped by then the trip would turn into a surprise visit to the mountains with Bill and Deena showing him and Lucy their new home as Bill spun a wild tale of his adventures. But something in his gut twisted with anxiety. Bill was almost two decades older than Lucy and definitely more than twice as cautious... no way he went missing for a day without something being very, very wrong.

Nick made arrangements for the neighbor to keep the dog and feed the cat, did a quick load of laundry, made sure the dishwasher was run, so when they left in the morning—at five-thirty, which actually was about the time they both were up and on their way out most days—there'd be nothing left to do. He finished locking up the house and went upstairs to find Lucy packing while talking on the phone.

"Can the Civil Air Patrol help? And the Forest Service?" she was asking as she tucked a pair of her black cowboy boots into a suitcase, arranging them around the lockbox that held her guns. "And what about the charter pilots that take the hunters out? Don't some of them use infrared and thermal radar to stalk game? Right. Good." She turned to Nick and mouthed, "Deena."

Lucy pulled a black dress out of the closet and considered it with a frown. Prepared for the worst, that was her. She tossed it into the suitcase where it landed on top of her cargo pants and layers of outdoor garments. "Okay, sounds like your guys have all the bases covered. Our flight gets into Lewiston around one-thirty your time. We'll rent a car there. Of course it's no problem. And if he's home by the time we get there?" Lucy chuckled, but Nick could tell it was forced. "Then the steaks are on Bill. Besides, it's been ages since Nick and I took a trip, just the two of us. Deena, please. All right. You try to get some rest, and we'll get there as fast as we can. Call me if anything changes. Nick sends his love. Good night."

"How's she doing?" Nick asked once she hung up.

"Her sister and mom are coming down from the reservation but won't get there until tomorrow. They'll stay with her at the house. She's booked us into a motel."

"Yeah, but how is she?"

Lucy's mouth tightened. "She says all those years in Denver as a cop's wife, waiting for him to come home, she never felt like this. Back in the city, if something happened, you'd know it. There'd be the knock on the door and the other wives gathered and the guys escorting you to the hospital and waiting to give blood;

you'd never be alone. But out there, in Magruder—"

"It's just her alone in the house, and nothing but waiting without any answers."

"Not totally alone. The local veterinarian—"

"Judy? The one whose husband bought her the motel that came with a zoo? Bill made her sound like some kind of hippie-love child. Not sure how well she and Deena get along."

"Judith," Lucy corrected him. "And from what Deena says, I think she'd almost rather be alone instead of being hovered over. Especially, as it turns out, since Judith is the closest thing they have to a medical doctor, she's also the county coroner."

"So while Judith is watching over Deena, Deena's watching over her—"

"Because if Judith gets a call-out, it won't be good news." Lucy grimaced.

"I'm glad we're going." They stood side by side for a long moment. Then Nick began to fill his own suitcase. His outdoor clothes weren't as military-inspired as Lucy's, but the whole family was avid hikers, so he had a fair selection. "What's the weather like there?"

"It's August, so pretty hot during the days but down to the forties at night, and colder at elevation," Lucy answered. "Good thing for the search parties—it stays light until around eight-thirty. As long as he has water and isn't hurt, he'll be fine." She sounded more like she was trying to convince herself than Nick.

"What was he doing when they heard from him last? Was he out on a call? Serving a warrant?"

"Deena said the last people to see him were some farmers about a bear on their land. He called it in to the forest service folks and left. No one's seen or heard from him since."

"Except you."

"Except me. And I was at the doctor's getting a CAT scan and X-rays, and had my phone off." She pulled a dark suit from his closet, but shook her head.

"Too formal, even if—" Nick left the sentence unfinished. "Jeans and a button-down. Works either way, celebration or..."

She nodded and returned the suit to the closet.

"Don't forget a bathing suit," he reminded her.

"And just when are we going to have time to go swimming?"

"The hot springs. Bill said that's where the whole town hangs out half the time, at least when the tourists aren't around. His first two cases after he became sheriff were solved sitting in the water, listening to the gossip."

"Cases," she scoffed. "A guy shot an elk out of season, and a kid stole a pony-keg of beer from the church bingo game. The man worked major crimes for eleven years."

"He loved it, being back where he grew up. Being close to Deena's family after the cancer." Deena had had breast cancer three years ago but luckily was in full remission. "Plus, he said it was so much healthier for the both of them. Peace and quiet, hiking in the mountains...God's country, he called it."

"Let's pray that he's just lost, hunkered down for the night. By the time we get there tomorrow, he'll have wandered back out, embarrassed and hungry."

Nick hugged her tight. Her body remained rigid with worry for a long moment before finally relaxing into his embrace. Bill simply being lost was the best-case scenario.

But they both knew it was the least likely.

Chapter 5

Deena was waiting. He couldn't keep her waiting... No, she was here, he could hear her voice, the wind shifting it hither and yon, teasing him. Where was she?

Bill tried to open his eyes, but only one seemed to work. His head thundered with the effort, and he immediately closed it again. Pain, everywhere, so intense he couldn't localize where it was coming from, couldn't think, couldn't breathe.

What? Where? The questions floated like balloons, the wind carrying them out of reach.

He tried to call to Deena; she'd know the answers, she'd save him. But all that emerged was a primal grunt.

Memory crept into his awareness, like a ghostly fog, easily blown away and scattered into nothing. An electrical shock. His heart stopping then racing, thudding against his chest. Weightless, flying, falling. Muscles locked, spasming, no chance to breathe, to stop, to catch himself... limbs flailing, scraping against scree and shards of granite... something snapping, more pain, the crunch of bone, the thud of unprotected soft parts... God, this headache! If it would just stop for a minute, let him think, let him remember...

He lay there for a long moment, fighting his way clear of the tangled skein of half-formed memories. Then his training took over. If the past was a blur, no matter, forget about it; he needed to focus on the now.

Take inventory. He wasn't falling, not any more. That was good. He lay twisted, could feel rock pressing against his head—which still pounded like a howitzer—his back, his right side, his legs... His legs, his legs!

He didn't even have words to describe the agony radiating from his legs. Worse than his head—no, not worse, just different. And wet; they felt wet. Had he pissed himself? Was he lying in water? His face was wet, too. Was he drowning?

Fear overwhelmed the pain, and his one good eye popped open. He was lying in shadow, wedged between a large boulder and the cliff wall, but beyond was the night sky with a moon bright enough to make him blink. ABC, he told himself. Airway; yeah, that was working. Breathing; hurt like a sonofabitch, but he was doing it. Circulation and C-spine. Lie still in case his back was broken? His right arm was pinned beneath him, and he couldn't feel it at all. His left was free. He wiggled his fingers; they worked, that was good. He inched his hand to his face, skimming his body as if afraid if he let his hand drift out of his sight it might vanish altogether. Every movement, every touch no matter how light, hurt. He touched his face. Right cheek caved in, eye swollen and sticky with blood that was still flowing.

The effort exhausted him and he closed his good eye, his good hand resting on his chest, making sure he didn't forget to keep breathing. A stray memory from Denver drifted past slowly enough for him to catch it: a skydiver, whose chute failed, broke most every bone in her body but still lived to tell the tale.

He hadn't fallen a tenth as far as she had, he chided himself. And no one was coming to help, not anytime soon. *God helps them that helps themselves*, a man's voice—Dad?—scolded him.

Bill struggled to open his eye again. He felt exhausted and cold; why was it so cold? The sun had set but the temperature had to still be in the sixties at least. His head felt too heavy for his body; he'd never be able to sit up. But his legs felt wet, more than water, and numb like two dead logs attached to his hips. Even the pain had fled, chased away by the cold gray creeping damp.

Phone? He flapped his left hand against his shirt pocket. No phone. It was gone. He'd have to do this the hard way.

He braced his good arm against the boulder and slowly, his breath coming in gasps that were daggers stabbing through his ribs, he untwisted his torso, raising his head and chest enough to prop himself against the stone wall. His right hand was white, the blood squeezed out by the weight of his body on it. Pins and needles and then a sharper pain that brought a hoarse scream when he tried to place any weight on it. Worse than the pain was the feeling of bone scraping against bone.

Bad, but it wouldn't kill him. Focus, focus. His vision wavered, trying to recreate the illusion of depth perception with one eye, and he shifted his attention to his legs. Nausea roiled through him, his entire body chilling at the sight. His left shin was deformed, both bones obviously broken, with his kneecap aimed one way and the toes of his boot aimed another. Even worse was the large puddle of blood oozing from a deep puncture wound on the thigh of his other leg. His entire right leg felt shortened and was hopelessly skewed at an unnatural angle, the hip bone no longer properly connected to the thigh bone.

Somewhere in the black recesses of his

mind, he knew he should be feeling a lot—a hell of a lot—more pain, but that creeping chill numbness was even more frightening. *Shock. Shock will kill you. Fast. Move, move, move.*

No matter how much he screamed commands inside his head, he only had one working hand, and it wasn't the one his belt was designed to accommodate. It took several efforts to remove his belt—thankfully it wasn't a complicated patrol officer's duty belt, just a normal man's belt, since all he carried on most calls were his service weapon and a pair of handcuffs. His holster was empty—Lord only knew where his gun had landed—but the leather pouch with the cuffs was there; he was lucky it hadn't jammed into his spine, caused any damage. With fingers fumbling with urgency and shock, he slid the handcuff pouch free and wrapped the belt twice around his thigh above the break and the bleeding. It took three tries to thread the end through the buckle.

Then he yanked it tight. As tight as he could. A shriek of pain escaped him, echoing across the canyon and ricocheting from the cliff walls, hurtling right back at him.

He never heard it, the tsunami of pain pulling him back into the void.

Chapter 6

BECAUSE OF THEIR LATE BOOKINGS, Lucy spent all three of their flights on opposite ends of the plane from Nick. Which, in a way, was a bit of a relief. She still hadn't told him about what the surgeon wanted to do—mainly because she still wasn't sure what *she* wanted to do or how she felt about what the surgeon wanted to do. Every time she tried to think about it, her mind blurred with frustration, fear, and an overwhelming sense of failure. She'd worked so hard after losing her job with the FBI, she'd almost convinced herself that her new life was everything she wanted, that she was back to normal.

What did Nick always say? *Denial, it's not*

just a river in Egypt...

If she had the amputation, she had a better chance of being able to stay in the field, and would be almost fully functional again. And one thing she was certain of was that she didn't want to give up fieldwork.

But it came at a price. Not just losing a part of herself; the price her family paid for her continuing her job. Maybe getting her life back to normal wasn't the best thing for them.

Except...who was she then? A forty-year-old woman starting over...as what? A desk jockey reviewing cases? That wasn't her; she'd go crazy within a week.

Maybe what she needed to decide wasn't whether or not she wanted the surgery, but how much was she willing to sacrifice to keep doing the job she loved.

Instead of trying to solve her own life, she focused on the search for Bill. Using the planes' Wi-Fi, she downloaded maps of Magruder County. What a crazy patchwork of jurisdictions! Poet Springs sat literally at the end of the only paved highway leading into Magruder

County—if you could call what Google Earth revealed to be a narrow, twisting two-lane road a "highway." The county seat was virtually surrounded on all sides by federal lands: the Nez Perce National Forest, Selway-Bitterroot Wilderness, Bitterroot National Forest, and Frank Church-River of No Return Wilderness. When she zoomed in on the map, she saw traces of dirt roads through the national forest, including a route that ran west to east, bisecting the two wilderness areas. Magruder Corridor it was labeled on some maps, Nez Perce Trail on others.

Bill was responsible for patrolling and maintaining order on what was basically an old pioneer stagecoach trail, Lucy realized. Knowing Bill, he loved that idea. She could see the appeal—and the challenge for a law enforcement officer.

Deena had said Bill's patrol SUV, an ancient Jeep Cherokee, was too old to have GPS, and the county was too poor to upgrade the three official sheriff's department vehicles.

"The nearest cell tower is Elk City, so that

didn't narrow things much as far as a search radius. Bill wants to get satellite phones for the department, but that's in next year's budget," Deena told Lucy when she called from the Salt Lake City airport while Nick found them lunch.

"What about his phone's GPS? That should work even without cell reception."

"The last place it registered was near the Holmstead ranch, his last call. I guess his phone must have died. He'd never have turned it off."

Unless he didn't want to be tracked—or someone else didn't want him found. Lucy frowned at what Nick called her "catastrophic thinking." It was a bad habit, all her pessimism and negative thoughts bordering on paranoia, so she was trying her best to be more positive. "He didn't radio in a location?"

"Not after he left the Holmsteads. They were the last people to see him." Her voice broke, but she pulled herself together. "The forest service is helping to coordinate the ground search. The civil air patrol is already out. The K9 team from Missoula will be here later today, and more volunteers are coming from all over."

"Sounds like everything possible is being done." The words sounded lame as soon as Lucy said them. Nick approached with two bags of fast food just as the gate agent announced that boarding was starting. "I have to go. We'll be there soon, so whatever you need. Did your mom and sister get there yet?"

Deena gave a laugh that was half a sigh. "If you were here, you'd smell the tea and the sage and the laundry and the floor wax and the baking. I actually brought the phone out to the deck; I can't take their hustling and hovering. It's worse than when I was sick. It's like they're trying to scrub out any trace of him, prepare me for him not coming back." A sob escaped her.

Lucy was half tempted to hand the phone off to Nick. "Deena—"

"No, no. I'm okay. Catch your flight, and I'll see you soon." She hung up.

A few minutes later, she and Nick were on another plane—their third of the day, each one smaller than the last. This one was a tiny twelve-row commuter, with two seats to one side of the aisle and a single seat on the other. Which meant Lucy was alone as she poured over her maps, trying to memorize landmarks, orient herself, figure out the best way to search for Bill.

Ever since she was a kid, Lucy had been fascinated by maps. Growing up, her bedroom had been decorated by large NOAA maps her father had found at a yard sale. And back when Lucy was on the Critical Incident Response Team at the FBI Academy in Quantico, she'd done research on Geographic Information Systems and had developed a way to use them to track serial offenders. It was what had helped her catch Clinton Caine, the sadistic serial killer, when until then his crimes had never been connected to one man. A friend of hers with the US Marshal Service had even adapted her algorithm to use in searches for escaped fugitives.

But now as she stared at screen after screen of maps of Magruder County, she worried that she couldn't be of any help at all in the search for Bill. He wasn't hiding, wasn't on the run, wasn't obscuring his tracks. Yet it had been almost twenty-four hours and no one had found his patrol vehicle or any trace of him.

Her eyes blurred as she zoomed in on a topographical map, noting how densely stacked the lines indicating a change in altitude were. This was steep, rugged country. She zoomed out and was quickly lost in a sea of green: light green for national forest, dark green for the designated wilderness areas. A few scattered islands of white for private land. A ribbon of blue for the Salmon River and its major forks—surrounded by black topo lines. Bill had told her that the canyon the river formed was even deeper than the Grand Canyon.

It was no better when she switched to satellite and photographic views. In fact, it was worse. These Bitterroot mountains weren't anything like her Alleghenies, gentle and as well-worn as an old quilt. No, these mountains climbed to snow and stone-capped peaks sharp as daggers piercing the sky. Despite hundreds of years of human trespass pillaging their gold and logs and other natural treasures, they refused to be tamed. This wasn't the Idaho of potato farms and cattle ranches. This was a wild frontier.

And somewhere in that unrelenting sea of green, Bill was lost or hurt or being held against his will... or dead.

Chapter 7

Once Nick and Lucy arrived in Lewiston, Nick headed in search of a car rental while Lucy stood in line with burly men claiming rifle cases and fishing poles from the special luggage office. Before he got far, he spotted a woman holding a sign with Lucy's name on it. She was in her mid to late fifties with copper-red hair pulled back in a youthful ponytail.

"Mr. Guardino?" she asked as Nick approached. Under other circumstances, he would have corrected her: because of Lucy's work, she used her maiden name, and technically Nick was Dr. Callahan. But under these circumstances, he really didn't care what anyone called him.

"Yes, hello. I'm Nick, Lucy's husband."

"Judith Keenan." She extended her hand and he shook it.

This was Judith? The veterinarian slash county coroner? What was she doing here? "Did you find Bill? Is he okay?"

"I'll be flying you to Poet Springs."

"Flying?" Lucy asked as she joined him, her suitcase with her guns at her side.

"Lucy, this is Judith. Judith Keenan, Bill's friend." Nick made introductions. He turned back to Judith. "Shouldn't you be out helping to search for Bill?"

Lucy shushed Nick with a glance, and he realized that if the search had progressed to where it didn't need every pilot available, then it was no longer a rescue mission, but a recovery.

"Where did they find his body?" Lucy asked.

The woman did a double-take. "No, I'm sorry. I have my own plane, a little Cessna 206, but it doesn't have thermal tracking like some of the charter pilots, so I volunteered to pick up two of their clients, and thought I'd save you time as well. Is that a problem?"

Nick recovered first, as Lucy exhaled and closed her eyes for a long moment. "Yes, thank you, Judith. That was very thoughtful of you. Didn't Deena tell me you were the county coroner? I guess it's a good thing they don't need you back home." He winced at his own feeble attempt at humor.

Judith didn't seem to notice. She led the way out to the tarmac where several small planes were waiting. In front of one paced two men, both in their late thirties, one broad-shouldered with a pock-marked face and the other thin with clothes that hung too large from his frame as he clutched a large black Pelican case on wheels.

Nick took their suitcase from Lucy and joined the men while Judith opened the plane's clam-shell doors. There were large canisters labeled "Pro-min Llama Mineral Supplements" along with bags of herbivore and omnivore pellets already stacked in the narrow cargo area. Nick glanced at the other passengers' luggage, assessing if it would fit. The large Pelican case had the insignia of a North Dakota mining company and was labeled "Ground Penetrating Radar, Portable Unit" above a tracking barcode. GPR—Lucy used that when she was with the FBI to find old graves. What were these men looking for? he wondered.

Judith was obviously used to loading her tiny plane, because she packed all their luggage in the rear except for the bulky GPR unit, which she strapped into one of the four passenger seats in the middle compartment. "One of you will need to ride up front with me."

"I will," Lucy volunteered, as Nick and the two men climbed into the back.

"I'm Nick," he said by way of introduction to his two fellow passengers.

"Davenport," the thin man sitting across from him, one hand on the well-secured GPR unit. "That's Martin."

Martin took the seat beside Nick without even glancing in his direction.

"Ground penetrating radar." Nick nodded to the case. "What are you looking for?"

"Nothing in particular. Just a geological survey."

"You're geologists?"

"Geological engineers," Davenport corrected, sounding superior. "We don't just study rocks, we figure out how to dig them out."

Judith started the engine, and the noise drowned out any more conversation.

Once they had taken off, Nick settled into his seat, watching the landscape flow by beneath him. He'd never been in such a small plane before. It was noisy and rattled much more than a commercial jet. But somehow that made the whole experience feel intimate, as if he and his fellow travelers were sharing an unique experience, separate from the rest of the world. At first the ground rolled past in flat yellow-green ribbons. There were few clouds, and since they were headed east, the sun behind them cast their shadow ahead of them. As if there were two planes, one dark, one light, racing to catch up with each other.

In the cockpit, Judith finished speaking to the tower and took off her headset. As she adjusted her controls, she reached past Lucy. "FBI, huh?" Her voice was raised to carry over the noise of the engine. "You must have some stories."

Lucy's reply was muffled, but Nick was more interested in the two men sitting with him. The fellow beside him, the one with the beard, Martin, had flinched a little at Judith's mention of the FBI, his hand pulling up to adjust his seatbelt. Almost as if he were reaching for a gun? Nonsense. They were engineers, not criminals. And everyone felt nervous around cops—especially FBI agents, even retired ones. He glanced at the man opposite, Davenport. The thin man's face was a blank; but almost too blank. Huh. Usually Lucy's former profession provoked interest at the very least.

"Geological survey," he tried to start his own conversation. "Is that for the government? They're not looking to start fracking or drilling for oil out here, are they?"

Martin glared at Nick, silently telling him to mind his own business. It was a look Nick got a lot from new clients when he pushed them past their comfort zone.

"Private landowner," Davenport answered. The smile he directed at Nick was probably meant to be charming but fell short of the mark. "But it's really just a working vacation—an excuse for a fishing trip with a few hours of work thrown in on the side."

"Nice," Nick said, wishing he and Lucy had the same luxury. Wouldn't it be wonderful if they'd found Bill by the time they arrived, and they could turn it into a vacation? It had been a long time since he and Lucy had had one—since the last time they'd gone on a trip with Bill and Deena two years ago, following Sherman's March from Atlanta to Savannah.

"What are you looking for?" he asked Davenport. Bill had told him legends of gold still yet to be mined from the Bitterroots. "Gold?"

Davenport shook his head. "Nothing so exotic. Anyway, no one would use GPR to find gold to mine. But I really can't discuss a client's private business. You understand." He turned away to gaze out his window.

Nick didn't blame the engineer for being

more interested in the view. As they moved east, the landscape changed dramatically; rolling hills gave way to a wide expanse of forest climbing up increasingly steep mountains until at the far edge of the horizon they crescendoed into jagged rocky peaks that shone white against the sky.

Still, something about the two engineers bothered him. "I didn't know anyone could own land past Poet Springs."

"Oh, yeah, there's a few grandfathered in," Judith answered from the cockpit. "It's kind of a patchwork of homesteads—even in the Frank. Totally isolated in the winter, hard enough to get to in the summer, but those who live there, they love it. Nothing could make them leave."

"The Frank?" Lucy asked. She glanced over her shoulder at Nick, checking in. He gave her a smile.

"Frank Church-River of No Return Wilderness Area. The most remote region in the entire lower forty-eight." She sounded proud of the distinction.

Nick perked up at that. "River of No Return? Any good whitewater rafting?"

With Lucy starting her new job at Beacon Falls and his work at the VA picking up, they hadn't had a chance to even make it over to the Yough this summer for a rafting trip, much less anyplace exotic. Then he sobered, thinking of how Bill and Deena had postponed their visit because of work. It was far too easy to let opportunities slip away. After almost losing Lucy in January—hell, after almost losing her too many times to count, and those were only the situations she'd told him about—he'd vowed not to let that happen to them; yet here they were, their first trip together in years, and it was to search for a missing friend...or, most likely, recover his body.

"Yes, sir," Judith answered. "In fact, the ranch Mr. Davenport and Martin are headed to sits on the Salmon. It's a base camp for fishing, rafting, hunting—about any expedition you might want. As long as you don't mind llamas."

"I thought I saw you loading llama food."

"No motorized ground vehicles are

allowed in the wilderness areas, so you need anything, you got to fly it, float it in by river, or pack it in. The Holmsteads, they been raising llamas for decades. Great pack animals and more friendly to the environment than horses or mules."

"So people hunt from llamas?" There went his romantic vision of a cowboy on a horse in the woods sighting his rifle on a grizzly bear.

"No one hunts from on top of an animal—you need control. After all, you're responsible for every bullet you send out there. But as pack animals, to get you into extreme areas where the hunting is more challenging and more rewarding, you can't beat llamas."

"I'm surprised you don't mind hunting," Lucy put in. "Aren't you the local veterinarian?"

"Veterinarian, coroner, resort owner, and thanks to my husband, rest his soul, I'm even a zookeeper. And with Bill missing, turns out I'm now sheriff—hopefully not for long. Honestly the only job I don't enjoy is the zoo. Animals locked in cages. But they're all old, orphaned from circuses and carnivals that went under or bought by rich people who thought an exotic pet like a tiger cub was cute until it wasn't. Max, my husband, he had a soft heart and took them in; thought he was saving their lives. Me, I'm not so sure they wouldn't prefer to be put out of their misery."

Nick blinked. Judith did not sound at all like Dr. Rouff, their vet back home. But she was older, mid-fifties at least, so maybe she was speaking more from experience than sentiment.

"What do you mean, you're now sheriff?" Lucy asked.

"In Idaho if the elected sheriff can no longer perform his duties and hasn't appointed a replacement, the county coroner automatically assumes the office of sheriff. It was a surprise to me—never came up when Sheriff Langer had his heart attack because he already had Bill deputized as a reserve, and could ask him to step in. But now..."

"You're leading the search for the man whose job you now have?"

"I never said I wanted the job in the first place. Didn't even know it was a thing until

Judge Carson showed up at the search coordination meeting this morning and told me."

Outside Nick's window, he spotted a few buildings that appeared commercial, surrounded by some scattered houses and farms. "Is that Poet Springs?"

"No, that's Grangeville. Ten times the size of Poet Springs. And they have good cell service," Judith added, as a ringtone sounded. She reached past Lucy to grab a small leather case. "Must have gotten a text. Would you mind checking for me? In case it's about Bill?"

Nick watched as Lucy opened the case and drew out a pilot's logbook, a spiral bound set of navigation charts, and a cell phone. She tapped the cell phone and the screen lit up. It must not have been locked because suddenly her expression changed: surprise and delight.

"It's from Bill," Lucy announced.

"He's alive!" Judith said, glee sending her voice up a notch. "Thank the Lord! What's it say?"

"It's time-stamped twenty minutes ago.

But it's kind of weird." She hesitated and glanced at Nick before reading the text. "I'm sorry. Don't let D find me. Bill." She raised the phone closer to her face as if interrogating it. "That's it."

"Doesn't sound like Bill. Why wouldn't he want Deena to find him?" Judith asked. "I don't get it. But at least he's alive. And he must be somewhere within range of a cell tower, so we can see where he was when the text was sent."

Nick leaned back, ignoring the brilliant sky out his window and the shifting patterns the sunlight cast inside the cabin. He agreed with Judith—that text didn't sound like the Bill he knew. "Judith, could Bill be trying to hide something from Deena? Like an affair?"

"I doubt it—when he's around her is about the only time lately he's seemed happy. Something was getting him down, though, worrying him. Not sure if it was the job—if it was, it wasn't any case I was involved with as coroner, so I wouldn't know. He did mention needing a checkup before the election, so maybe he was sick and didn't want Deena to find out?"

She paused and adjusted a control. The plane shifted, rocked a tiny bit, then settled back level. "But why text me?"

Lucy turned to look at Nick. Now her face was filled with worry. "*Don't let D find me.* He's not talking about running away with another woman, is he?"

Nick had to force himself to meet her gaze. He suddenly felt heavy, almost surprised the tiny plane wasn't straining against the weight that collapsed his shoulders. "I don't think there's another woman. I think he meant that text for the new sheriff of Magruder County."

Her eyes widened, but she nodded slowly. Because the only reason Judith would be sheriff was if the old one was gone.

I'm sorry. Don't let D find me.

Sounded like the note of a desperate man.

Then he shook himself. There was no point jumping to conclusions—and plenty of people wrote messages like that without harming themselves. Maybe Bill just needed time alone to think.

No matter what, at least they knew that as of twenty minutes ago, he was alive.

Until he saw proof otherwise, that was exactly how Nick was going to continue to think about things. It was a search and rescue, now with a new starting place. Which meant hope. And if Bill needed help—Nick's particular kind of help—then it was a damn good thing he'd come along with Lucy. He was not about to lose a friend to that kind of darkness. He'd lost too many already.

Nick couldn't stop himself from glancing at Lucy. Because over these past few months, since her mother's murder, that awful night when the dog attacked and she'd almost died, there had been times when he feared he might lose her as well. Not just her body, but her soul.

No. They'd find Bill. Alive. And do whatever it took to help him.

And then...then he'd talk to Lucy. Get everything out in the open. He'd let her keep hiding her feelings from him—from herself—for far too long.

First Bill. Then Lucy.

CHAPTER 8

NOW THAT THEY KNEW BILL was alive—at least that he had been when he'd sent the text an hour ago—Lucy felt energized, a myriad ideas to help with the search filling her head. But she also dreaded what they might find. That text... Bill was fifty-nine; maybe he simply didn't express himself well in the shorthand that text messages demanded? He would know Judith would be involved in the search for him. Was he specifically trying to tell her something? Wanted to alert her somehow to something, get her to dig deeper?

Lucy had worked cases in plenty of less remote and more populated areas of the country where getting away with murder and other crimes was far easier than civilians imagined. Hell, right in her own backyard in rural Pennsylvania, she'd caught serial killers who'd been able to hunt for years without ever hitting law enforcement's radar.

It wasn't that the police didn't want to solve crimes or were incompetent; they simply had insufficient resources, inadequate manpower, and often lacked the training to get the job done. Despite what people saw on shows like *CSI*, normal community cops whose budget relied on taxpayers' whims faced enormous odds. It was to their credit that so few major felons escaped justice—the product of long hours, good instincts, and bulldog tenacity despite being overworked and underpaid.

Working at Beacon Falls, seeing the ever-growing queue of cold cases that families and law enforcement turned to Lucy's team to help solve, she'd come to realize that even heinous criminals often operated in plain sight. Now, watching Judith skillfully steer the plane around several mountain peaks as she circled them onto the flight path for the narrow landing strip at Poet Springs, Lucy's heart dropped at the sight of the miles and miles of unbroken wilderness stretching out in all directions, surrounding the tiny gathering of buildings that was the county seat. If someone didn't want to be found, Magruder County was definitely the place to vanish.

The runway and its Quonset-style hangar and small outbuildings sat at the western end of a narrow valley. About a mile away, nestled against the foothills that formed the valley's walls, sat another cluster of buildings: a large red barn-like structure with a peaked metal roof that was surrounded by small cabins; downhill from that along the main road were a whitewashed church, several buildings that sat shoulder to shoulder like Pittsburgh rowhouses but with western-style façades along their roofs, a gas station, and a brick building almost the same size as the church it sat opposite from. Lucy made a mental bet with herself that it was either a bank or a government building.

She'd been in small towns like Poet Springs all over the country, from West Texas to

Tennessee to her own Pennsylvania. She'd grown up in a town almost as small and isolated; she understood how these people thought, how they would come together in a time of crisis, how little they'd appreciate outside interference.

Judith had radioed ahead about receiving the text from Bill, so by the time they landed and taxied to a stop near a large Quonset hangar, Lucy half-hoped to be greeted by a hang-faced Bill himself. This was one occasion where she'd love to have her paranoid suspicions of foul play disproved.

Instead, they climbed out of the Cessna to find a battered white Econoline van waiting. The driver, a middle-aged Hispanic man, hopped out and immediately began unloading the plane's cargo, his only greeting a tip of his straw hat in Judith's direction. The two geological engineers grabbed their gear and climbed into the van while Judith finished taking care of the plane and had a quick conversation with the driver. Lucy shamelessly eavesdropped as Nick grabbed their bags.

"No word?" Judith asked him.

The man shook his head.

"Couldn't they use the text to locate the cell tower it came through?" Lucy asked. "They could try sending a silent SMS, ping his phone, see if it's still on, maybe triangulate from several towers. Or get his coordinates from his GPS signal?"

Both the man and Judith turned to glare at her. She backed away, reminding herself that she was a guest here, not an FBI agent—not even a retired one. Judith finished her conversation and rejoined Nick and Lucy. "Harriet, our dispatcher at the sheriff's office, forwarded the info about the text Bill sent me to the state police. They'd already contacted his cell carrier and they said it came through the same cell tower his other calls yesterday used. Makes sense, since it's the only one around here. Best they could do was narrow the search area by a few miles. Said his phone is off now, so they can't do much else."

"But the GPS?" Lucy asked.

"Shows he moved a bit to the east since

his last call yesterday—which was to you," Judith said, arching an eyebrow in Lucy's direction.

"I missed it," Lucy admitted. "He left a message asking me to call back."

Judith gave a hrumphing noise as if frustrated by Lucy's inability to help. "Well, he must have either turned his phone off after he called you or he was in one of the GPS dark spots—there's a bunch around here. Sometimes it can take fifteen-twenty minutes for a phone to pick up a satellite signal."

Nick carried their suitcase and daypacks to the waiting van, where the two engineers were waiting impatiently.

"I'll drop you two off at the hot springs," Judith told Lucy, "then Miguel can take Mr. Davenport and his partner here out to the Holmstead ranch."

"We want to join the search," Lucy protested.

Nick loaded their bags into the van, hopped in, and extended a hand to Lucy. She felt Judith's gaze on her so made a point of climbing in herself, hiding a wince of pain. Ten hours cramped into airline seats hadn't done her ankle any good.

Judith got into the passenger seat while Miguel resumed his spot in the driver's seat. She twisted in her seat to face the rear compartment. "Nick, you and Lucy can drop your bags and get geared up for the search, but I'm not sure where they'll assign you. Sheriff's office is coordinating and handling administration, but the forest service is in charge of the volunteers. It'll be up to them."

"Lucy," Nick said, "one of us should check on Deena." His tone implied that one should be her.

She shot him a glare. "Sounds like a job for a trauma counselor. You'd be much more comfort and help than I would be. I want to see where Bill's last location was, and talk to any witnesses."

"We've taken care of all that," Judith interjected. "We might not be the FBI, but we actually do know what we're doing."

"But with the text he sent today, the

timeline changes," Lucy protested, until Nick squeezed her knee and she shut up.

Miguel steered the van down a rain-washed gravel road leading away from the airstrip and into town. The drive took all of five minutes but was noisy enough that it precluded any further conversation. Lucy won the bet with herself—the large brick building had the insignia of a defunct bank carved into its cornice, but now housed various government offices including the sheriff's department. She also spotted a café, a general store, a diner, and a hunting-fishing outfitter. Despite it being tourist season, the only people she saw were a couple sitting at the café's outdoor tables. Finally, at the end of the road, they parked in front of the large barn-like building nestled into the curve of the mountains.

"Welcome to the Keenan Hot Springs and Exotic Wild Animal Exhibit," Judith said. "I've put you all in cabin three. Come inside and we'll get your keys."

Nick and Lucy grabbed their bags and followed her inside the massive building. It was three stories high at its peak, and as soon as they crossed the threshold, there was the distinctive scent of sulfur.

“The smell’s from the hot springs,” Judith said, as she meandered around a registration desk. Moose and elk heads featuring sprawling antlers adorned the walls along with other trophies: bears, wolves, mountain lions, bighorn sheep. “You can access them from inside, down that hallway through the shower and changing rooms, or from outside at the rear of the building.” She grabbed two old-fashioned metal keys on large key fobs from the pegboard. A raucous shriek echoed through the space followed by the flutter of wings and several bright green feathers floating out of the sky. Lucy glanced up to see three colorful parrots perched in the rafters above them. “Come on, I’ll show you to your cabin. The zoo’s on the other side of the building—right now we’ve got a tiger, a three-toed sloth, two ocelots, and a grizzly. Used to have a lion and a snake exhibit, but they’re gone.”

“Gone?” Nick asked. “You said the

animals were orphans; did you find homes for them?"

Judith's smile never faltered. "Gone as in dead. The lion from old age, the snakes after they killed my husband."

Chapter 9

They followed Judith through the massive grand hall, suitcases rattling across wide plank floors, the parrots tumbling from one rafter to the next, following them. At the rear of the hall was a dining area, but before that Judith turned down the corridor opposite the one leading to the hot springs.

"If you need anything, my apartment is behind the registration desk," she told them. Her voice echoed through the cavernous space. "We're hosting a cookout tonight for the searchers—sunset is around eight-thirty, so they'll all be in from the field after that. Might get noisy; we're suddenly full up, with all the volunteers come over from Darby and Missoula.

Good thing Deena warned me you were coming, so I saved you a cabin."

"How many rooms do you have?" Nick asked.

"We have eight cabins and a bunkhouse out back plus rooms above each wing. When they built this place back in the forties, they thought there'd be another east-west highway, but then they decided Route 12 up north was enough. Now the only time we're ever full is times like this. Of course I comp the volunteers their rooms, so that's not much help, but we're still hanging on."

"So you have searches fairly often?"

"A few times a season. Most don't last more than a few hours, a day at most, and we handle things locally, but this time we mobilized everyone fast. Bill isn't some tenderfoot tourist who doesn't know better than to rely on their smartphone to get them out of trouble. Someone as experienced as he is goes missing, we take it seriously."

The corridor opened up into another wide space, the ceiling not as high as in the lobby.

The three walls were almost all windows, and sunlight streamed in to capture dust motes floating like snowflakes. In the center of the end wall was a large glass enclosure with trees and bushes and a large creature hanging from one of the trees, its fur a strange silver-green. The sloth. She'd never seen one in person. It didn't move, to all appearances asleep. Beside it in a similar enclosure Lucy spotted a small spotted cat—one of the ocelots.

To their left were glass aquariums, all empty, the former home of the executed snakes, Lucy surmised. She sniffed and held back a sneeze; the place had a musty smell, thicker and more acrid than any barn back home. Then the noise of something big moving had her spinning to her right, her hand going to her hip where her weapon should have been. Her entire body went rigid as adrenaline flooded her, the sense of danger overwhelming. For a moment she was trapped in that night eight months ago, the dog's weight pinning her down. In her panic she took a step back, scanning the area, certain the dog was there, ready to pounce, waiting for her.

Nick was ahead of her, peering over a waist-high railing. She joined him, not because she was interested in the view but because her need to protect him overrode her fear.

Below them were two large pits, outfitted with boulders and small trees and bushes. The outside wall was solid glass so that people could observe the animals down at their level, providing a more intimate view. Yet, even though she was farther away, a good fourteen feet above where the two predators paced, Lucy somehow felt more exposed. There was no glass, no bars between her and two creatures engineered for killing.

It was difficult to focus on either one of them as her pulse ratcheted. She slid her body between Nick and the railing—he didn't seem to notice as he turned to keep talking to Judith, his back to the beasts. The tiger sprawled over a boulder, basking in a beam of sunlight as it licked its front claws. It stared straight at Lucy, assessing the distance, the strength it would take to leap it. Lucy shivered, unable to break away from the cat's hypnotic gaze.

Then the grizzly made a snuffling noise—nowhere near a growl but enough to make the hairs on Lucy's arms quiver in anticipation. She sniffed, the scent so like the dog who haunted her nightmares—the stench of her own fear or their predator excitement? The grizzly shuffled to the center of its enclosure where it could see these new humans most clearly, then with a grace surprising in such a massive creature, popped up from four legs to two, revealing its full height. Its nose scented the air and it sniffed loudly.

"Tabby and Smokey," Judith made the introductions. "My husband's legacy. At least what remains of it."

"He gave you a zoo," Nick whispered in awe, walking in a circle, taking in the space.

"He gave me a zoo." Judith's chuckle was laced with sorrow. "Max was a dreamer. Everyone loved him. And how that man could make me laugh. This," she spread her arms wide, "was his idea of retirement from life in the big city. He wanted to make this old place a tourist destination; dreamed of inviting world-class chefs and performers. Of adding a full-service health spa to go along with the hot springs. That was Max. A dreamer."

"Where did you live before?" Nick asked.

Lucy couldn't tear her gaze away from the animals. She took deep breaths, cleansing the adrenaline from her body. *Nothing to be afraid of, no need to panic.* Slowly her body began to believe her subliminal mantra.

She'd encountered black bears while hiking back home, but although she'd always been wary and respectful, she'd never felt this sense of...awe. And sadness. Tabby and Smokey were obviously well cared for, but they just seemed so lonely. Even more than at a real zoo, they seemed out of place here, like trophies that simply hadn't been stuffed and mounted yet.

"Chicago," Judith answered. "But one day Max got mugged. And he was getting older—he was sixty-four back then. So he came up with a new dream. For us." She shook her head. "That's how Max made his fortune, you know. Dreaming. Businesses would call him in, he'd shadow the managers, eat in the company cafeteria, listen to the gossip, examine the sales figures and manufacturing plants, whatever, and he'd come back with ideas to increase productivity and profits, ideas for new products, new markets. One visit from Max and he could save your company. But he couldn't save this place. Couldn't see that a falling down motel at the end of a road going nowhere would never attract anything more than broke backpackers. They don't want glamour and gourmet food, they want flush toilets and real meat instead of dehydrated crap. And after seeing real nature and wildlife up close and personal, the last thing they want is to see animals trapped behind bars. Coming here, it broke him. Even before the accident."

"You said—a snake?" Nick's tone was soft, a gentle breeze opening a door to someone's psyche. Lucy knew he sensed Judith's wound and was giving her a chance to release some of her pain.

Neither of them probably even remembered Lucy was standing right there or that they were in a hurry to join the search for

Bill. Nick could do that—make you feel like time had stopped, that nothing else mattered except whatever you needed to say. It was a gift, but it also sometimes drove her a bit crazy. But she couldn't leave him here, not alone with the animals, no matter how well they were contained. It made no sense, she knew, but that didn't matter.

Judith nodded to the empty enclosures across the room. But she didn't look at them, instead turning her body so her back was to them. "I was gone, out all night at the Holmsteads' helping deliver a baby alpaca. Turns out, coming here I'm busier than ever as a veterinarian, but it's all making house calls, and a lot of them pretty far away. That's why I got my pilot's license."

She took a deep breath. "Anyway, we're not sure how it happened. Miguel came in the next morning to find Max dead. The coroner over in Idaho County found a tiny puncture wound on his hand. He'd been cleaning the enclosures, and must have gotten careless. The coral snake, they finally decided—their bites are painless, so he probably never even realized. The snakes were supposed to have had their venom glands removed when Max bought them—although he was still careful, of course, and treated them with respect. Because you can never be a hundred percent sure…" Her voice lowered to a whisper. "Of anything. Of having a dream come true. Of coming home to your husband."

"But you're still keeping his dream alive," Nick told her. "Was it your dream as well?"

She shrugged. "At first I wanted to sell, but no one wanted to buy. As a veterinarian, I can't in good conscience keep these animals in captivity, but, just like me, they're trapped. They have nowhere else to go. So, I guess now I'm just waiting for them to die. Then I'll see what's next for me."

Lucy finally broke in. "Must keep you busy, running this place and your veterinary practice and being county coroner." She paused. "And now acting sheriff…"

Judith took the hint. "Right. Of course." She was all business again—except for the way she gazed at Nick, a strange combination of gratitude and worship in her eyes. Lucy had seen that look before, all too often. Good thing Nick was impervious to it, even if Judith wasn't at least fifteen years older than he was. "Right through here," she opened the door leading outside, "and up that path. You're in cabin three. I'll be leaving in ten minutes if you want to join the search or need a ride to Bill's home."

"Thanks, Judith. We won't be long." Nick turned to her, glancing behind him at the zoo. "I think Max would be proud of the way you're honoring his dream while also finding your own."

Judith's gaze softened, then she turned and strode away, her left hand with its wedding ring tapping the railing above the tiger and bear.

CHAPTER 10

THE GUEST CABINS WERE ARRANGED in a semi-circle between the mountain and the main building, leaving them in perpetual shadow. Cabin three was just that: a one-room log cabin with a tin roof and tiny porch barely wide enough to fit two rocking chairs. Nick unlocked the door and they went inside, depositing their luggage on one of the two double beds. There was a battered dresser, some photos of wildflowers and whitewater rapids on the walls, no TV, a single lamp on the nightstand between the beds, and a curtained alcove that led to a dressing area and a bathroom.

Mindful of the time, Lucy didn't bother unpacking except to retrieve her weapons: one

Beretta 9mm in a paddle holster concealed at the small of her back and the other strapped to her ankle, a Kershaw Ken Onion knife in her front pocket, and a multi-tool in her backpack. She also took the collapsible walking stick Nick had given her—it reminded her the ASP baton she'd used as an FBI agent, but was thicker and with a push of a button extended from eight inches to forty-two, perfect for hikes in the woods when she needed to protect her ankle from rough terrain.

"Judith, she's—" Lucy shrugged, not sure of the right adjective, but Nick nodded his understanding as he checked his own pack to make sure he had everything he needed. She stroked the paracord bracelet Megan had given her—her touchstone—and pushed the unspoken issue. "That's why you should stay with Deena. I'll join in the search."

Even though his back was turned, she sensed his smile. He knew exactly what she was really talking about. "I didn't realize how steep and rocky it was out here."

"A hill's a hill; just keep going until you

reach the top." Although they both knew it wasn't going up that was the dangerous part for Lucy—it was the coming down, especially given the scree fields, remnants of rockslides wide enough that they'd been visible from the air as they flew in. "I'll be fine."

He said nothing, simply filled their water bottles and handed Lucy hers. She slid it into its holster on the waistband of her pack and hoisted the pack to her shoulder. She was used to living out of her go-bag, but given the needs of a search and rescue were quite different than law enforcement or an investigation, it actually weighed less now than usual. No Kevlar, no extra ammo—technically she shouldn't even be carrying into wilderness areas, but she felt naked without her guns—and she'd left space for maps and any rescue gear the search team might need her to carry.

They headed back out the door and down the hill to the main building. Lucy led them around the opposite way than they had come, avoiding the zoo. She didn't want to be anywhere near the animals. The alternative route gave them a chance to see the hot springs side of the building. Lucy was surprised. Instead of the Old Faithful type of basin she'd imagined, it was a regular concrete pool enclosed by glass walls and a peaked ceiling. The water gave off a sulfur smell and there was a haze of steam above its slightly greenish surface, but other than that she'd never know it was anything but a normal swimming pool.

Judith was right: this place was not the fairytale dream her late husband had envisioned. An eagle's shadow crossed Lucy's path, and she glanced up...and up and up, her gaze searching for the top of the mountain peak towering over them. Her vision filled with more shades of green than she could name. The air smelled of pine sap and the subtle honey scent of wildflowers, while the sky stretched out even wider than the mountain crags, promising infinity.

No manmade attraction could ever compete with this beauty. No wonder Bill loved it here.

Nick reached the van before Lucy did.

Judith was waiting, watching as Lucy used her walking stick to swing into the van without putting excessive weight on her ankle. She thought she managed it quite gracefully, no stumble or hint of weakness, but Judith still frowned as she slammed the door and made her way to the driver's seat.

They followed a paved road east. A few miles out of town the pavement abruptly stopped, giving way to a well-packed dirt road with gravel ground into its surface. Another two miles and Lucy spotted a group of vehicles parked, blocking the narrow road. They ranged from pickup trucks to Subarus to large SUVs. People gathered on the far side of them, listening to a man in a dark green Forest Service uniform. He was black, mid-twenties, and exuded a sense of authority.

"That's Gleason," Judith told them as she parked behind an ancient Bronco. "Local ranger. Knows these woods better than anyone."

"He's in charge of the search?" Lucy asked, knowing she'd have to make her case to him. She extended her walking stick, noting that several of the other volunteers gathered also had sticks of their own, ranging from elaborately carved staffs and ski poles to random branches.

"Yep," Judith answered, leading the way as they wove past the vehicles to where a gray-haired woman dressed in sheriff's department khakis sat on a truck bed, a sheaf of papers weighted down by a rock on one side, a topo map spread open on her other, colored with highlighted areas and scribbled notations. Behind her were an open laptop and a walkie-talkie. "But Harriet here is the power behind the throne." She raised a hand and caught Harriet's attention. "Harriet, this is Lucy and Nick. They're here to help—friends of Bill's from out east."

The last made Harriet squint in their direction, assessing them. Lucy stood straight, shifting her pack so it rested easily on her shoulders. Harriet nodded to Nick, but her lips thinned as she scrutinized Lucy. "You're the FBI agent."

"Yes ma'am," Lucy answered, not sure of

the right tack to take with Harriet.

Harriet made a grunting noise and thrust clipboards at Lucy and Nick. "Fill it out, bring it back, and we'll see what we can make of you."

Chapter 11

JUST LOOK AT ALL THESE SHEEP milling around. Makes me sick. All puffed up with self-importance, thinking they're going to be the one to play hero today. Idiots.

"All right, people," Gleason, the forest ranger in charge of the search yells. "Gather up." The crowd stops talking and surges toward him. Nothing he says will surprise me, so I pay attention to the people instead. "First of all, thanks to the volunteers from Liberty Lutheran for putting together the sack lunches. Let's give them a round of applause." Of course they all start clapping, as if trail mix and ham sandwiches were gourmet delicacies. "If you need extras, they're on the table near their van."

Movement at the edge of the crowd catches my eye. The FBI agent, Lucy. I cough to hide my smile. The way Bill talked about her, you'd have thought she walked on water. She's nothing like what he described. Cheeks hollowed out by exhaustion, shoulders tight in a constant flinch, a gimpy ankle—of all these sheep gathered here, if I had to cull the herd, I would choose her as the weakest of the bunch. FBI agent or not.

"Radios," Gleason was saying. "Check your batteries before you head back out. Harriet's got spares. If you damaged your radio or it's not working, she'll sign you out a new one. Oh, and people, these radios are for official communications. Which means everyone and anyone can tune into your channel. So let's keep the *personal* chat to a minimum." A ripple of laughter spreads through the crowd. "And yes, that means no booty calls to your girl on another team."

A pair of kids jostle another kid between them, his face bright red.

"As you know, we received some excellent news a short time ago. Acting Sheriff Keenan got a text from Bill. I can't share the contents of the message—" The crowd's cheers and applause interrupt him. He raises his hands and they quiet. "Knowing when the message was sent and an approximate location has shifted our search area slightly. So you'll be receiving updated maps and assignments. Do not leave until you get your new assignments. Team leaders, if you have people out in the field, be sure to get theirs and update them as soon as possible."

The sheep nod, all smiling.

"Now, we have approximately six hours of daylight left. Let's use those wisely, and bring Bill home. Thank you very much. Dismissed."

Another round of applause; I have no idea what for. But I clap and smile anyway, my attention on the FBI agent's husband who is weaving through the crowd, approaching Gleason. Most of the others simply plop down on the ground, waiting for their leaders to bring their new assignments. They'll be on their feet the next six hours, so they know enough to rest while they can. The FBI agent remains on the outer edge, skirting the clumps of chatterers pouring over maps, also making her way to Gleason, somehow timing it so she arrives at the same time as her husband.

"Nick Callahan and Lucy Guardino. We're friends of Bill and Deena's," the husband tells Gleason, shaking his hand.

The FBI agent lets her husband do the talking—probably a smart idea, because from what I've seen so far, he's better at it than she is. When she and Nick were signing in, filling out the volunteer paperwork, Harriet was trying to be polite, asking questions, and Lucy kept trying to brownnose her. You don't brownnose Harriet—she might be in her seventies, but she pretty much runs this place; has for decades, and she sees right through that crap. Lived here all her life, even though her children and grandchildren all moved away and her husband passed on years ago. She knows everything worth knowing. Well, almost everything. She's my eyes and ears—shares all the best gossip and comings and goings with me, never realizing that with a few stray words she might be condemning one of her neighbors.

I like to think of it as stalking my prey. Actually, to tell the truth, it's the most fun part—well, other than the getting away with murder part.

"Right," Gleason says. "Harriet says your paperwork is all in order." He clears his throat, eyeing both of them. "Nick, I have a team down a man—they're out in the field, but I'm set to go out and get them their new assignments. So if you don't mind riding with me?" He nods to his Forest Service pickup parked behind him. "Lucy," he clears his throat again, "you've already met Judith Keenan, right? She's headed back to Bill's house. How 'bout you go with her and coordinate with the family? That all right with you, Judith?"

"Of course."

No hesitation. I hate that. The way we all jump to, following the rest of the flock.

Except Lucy. She's not merely hesitating, she's holding an entire silent conversation with her husband. His eyes narrow the slightest bit, her lips tighten, but then she nods. "That would be fine." She hands her fancy walking stick to her husband. "Guess you'll be needing this more than me."

"Okay, then. Let's go find Bill." Gleason slides his hands together either wiping away dirt or silently applauding himself.

It's everything I can do not to smile as I watch the crowd scatter, off to their oh-so-important and oh-so-futile assignments. They're not going to save Bill. Not today. Not tonight. Not ever.

I've made certain of that.

CHAPTER 12

ONCE THE REST OF THE VOLUNTEERS were sorted and on their way, Nick joined Gleason in his truck, and they headed east on the dirt road. After a short distance, the road intersected another dirt road and narrowed from two lanes to one. There was a signpost pointing in a variety of directions, basically confirming that nothing was nearby, along with another large sign that further emphasized the fact that they were in the middle of nowhere.

CAUTION, it read. *NO SERVICES 113 MILES, 8-10 HOURS OF DRIVING TIME. NARROW MOUNTAIN ROAD. AXE, SHOVEL, BUCKET, AND POTABLE WATER ESSENTIAL AT ALL TIMES. PROCEED AT YOUR OWN RISK.* Below it was a list of prohibited vehicles and a map of the route, which from a distance appeared more like a coiled rattlesnake than a road.

"You guys take your warning signs seriously," Nick said.

"Wish the tourists took them as seriously—or bothered to read them at all," Gleason answered. The radio in the truck was tuned to the search channel, but chatter remained sparse.

"Are you from here?" Nick asked.

"Seattle. My mom's an orthopedic surgeon at Harborview, and my dad's a landscape architect. But my grandparents lived up in the mountains, so every chance I had as a kid, I was out of the city and up there in the woods."

"Do you work much with Bill?"

"Oh, yeah. We meet for coffee most weeks at least once or twice, especially during tourist season and hunting season—that's when most trouble happens, whether it's in town or on Forest Service land. I'm a law enforcement ranger, so he's also deputized me to help—kind of a mutual aid sort of thing. Good guy." He shook his head, the corners of his mouth turning down. "Have to tell you, I'm more than a bit worried. It's not like him, not calling Deena, not leaving word before heading out. He knows there are plenty of places around here where a cell or radio can't reach you, especially if he was heading east like his cell's GPS suggests. He would have called in a position—if only to avoid folks worrying and coming out to search."

"So you think he's more than just lost?" Nick couldn't help but think of the text Bill had sent Judith a few hours ago.

Gleason sighed. "I don't know what to think. But the sooner we find him, the better."

They pulled up to where a SUV was parked off the side of the road. A girl in her mid-twenties hopped out and approached the truck, smiling. "Hey, Gleason. Nothing to report here."

"Hi, Amy." The ranger smiled back. "Got a new volunteer for you, and some new maps and search coordinates. And lunch."

"Great. Ginny and the boys are headed

in."

Gleason grabbed a box from the back of his truck while Nick took his daypack and Lucy's walking stick. Then, with a wave, Gleason was gone. Amy hoisted the box of lunches, shaking off Nick's offer to help, and they sat down in the shade of a group of birch trees that lined a trailhead.

"George had to get home in time to feed the livestock," Amy told Nick, after quizzing him on his wilderness skills, checking his gear, and briefing him on radio protocols. "That's who you're replacing."

Nick swatted at mosquitos and biting flies, but never fast enough to scare them away. "Why aren't you out searching?"

"I am," she answered. "This position here, at the confluence of a trailhead, the road, and that gulley over there? It's a constraint position. I watch anyone coming in or out, and make sure no one gets past me. That way the search area has a limit more than just an imaginary grid on the map. It's important work." A hint of defensiveness entered her voice.

"But also boring."

She chuckled. "Boring as hell. Other than Ginny and her team, you're the first person I've talked to all day. But I can't go too far from the ranch—in case my Paps needs me."

"So this is your land?"

"My grandfather's. As far as you can see. It's been in the family over a hundred and fifty years. The road," she gestured to the width of packed dirt as if it were a bustling interstate, "was named after my great-great-great, go on back a few more generations, uncle. Lloyd Magruder. He was a merchant from California. He came out here to visit his brother, who was staking a gold claim and ended up selling supplies to miners. In 1863 he was headed back home when he was jumped by three strangers, robbed, and thrown over a cliff."

"Wow—your family must be one of the oldest around here other than the Nez Perce, of course."

"Nez Perce," she corrected him, pronouncing it *nezz purse.* "But yeah, we were some of the first who settled here. Along with the Beacheys."

"Bill's family?" Nick knew Bill had grown up here, but had no idea his family had roots here.

"Bill never told you? His great-great something, Hill Beachey, was Lloyd's best friend. He tracked those three killers all the way to San Francisco, dragged them back to Lewiston, and made sure they were hung for Lloyd's murder. It was the first execution—well, legal one—in Idaho's history. He became the county's first sheriff; brought law to these parts."

"That's some friend."

She nodded. "My guess? They were more than friends, but don't say anything like that around any of the older folk like my Paps. Or maybe friendship just had a different meaning back then—seems like things like honor meant more than they do now."

Nick glanced at her; she didn't seem old enough to be so cynical. "You don't think there's any honor in today's world?"

"If there were, I wouldn't have had to leave school to come and take care of Paps all on my own. Seems like no one else in the family gives a shit about him or what he wants. They all just want to lock him up in a home and steal his land, take away his dreams." She shook herself and gave Nick a half-smile, half-grimace. "Sorry. I don't mean to dump on you. Anyone ever tell you you're easy to talk to?"

"Occasionally." His smile was a full smile. Footsteps sounded from the path behind them, and a girl even younger than Amy appeared, trailed by two teenaged boys. They were covered with sweat and dirt and carrying packs and radios matching the one he'd strapped to his pack's hip belt.

"This our new guy?" the girl asked.

"Yep." Amy didn't stand up, just gestured to the water jug and cooler parked in the shade. The boys rushed over and dug in. Their arms were crisscrossed with scratches and bug bites. "Got some DEET if you want it."

"Oh, yeah." The girl sighed. "That would

be awesome." She tossed her water bottle to one of the boys to fill. "We covered G4 thru 7 and F3 through 5. No signs of anyone."

"Plenty of fresh bear scat," one of the boys added.

The girl rolled her eyes. "There's always plenty of bear scat this time year. Huckleberries; they love the huckleberries."

"So do I," the boy said, talking around a mouthful of ham and cheese and white bread. "We headed over past the burn next? Tons of huckleberries there."

The girl ignored him to turn her gaze on Nick. "I'm Ginny. This is my stupid little brother, Tim, and his friend, Alan." She didn't indicate which boy was which, as if it didn't matter.

"Nick, Nick Callahan."

"Good to meet you. Let me check in and get our new coordinates and we'll be headed out." She turned to the boys. "Eat and pee and get your shit together. We're out of here in five. Did you hear me? Five minutes."

The boys ignored her. Ginny unfolded a

large map, took the new smaller one Amy handed her, and sat down on the ground comparing the two, talking to someone on her radio. One of the boys brought her fresh water, a sandwich, and a protein bar, which she accepted without a word.

"She seems a bit young," Nick confided to Amy. "They all do."

"Gotta be fifteen to join Search and Rescue. Ginny's a freshman over in Boise, home for the summer. This is their sixth search this season. They know what they're doing. Follow their lead; you'll be fine."

Ginny finished talking on the radio and returned to where Amy and Nick were waiting. "Okay, the plan is to move east, over to grids K4 thru 8, and give them a straight run." She pointed on her map, and Amy circled the areas on her own map. There were an impressive number of grids with a single hash mark through them. Not bad for a day's work, Nick thought. These kids took their search and rescue seriously.

With Bill's life at stake, it was good to

know.

"Everyone ready? Let's go," Ginny said. She gestured to Nick to join her as she began walking down the road. He moved to walk beside her, and the boys quickly fell in behind her after grabbing one last sandwich.

"We'll pick up our new trail about half a mile down. Amy checked your gear?" Ginny asked.

"Yes."

"You ever done any SAR work?"

"No," Nick admitted.

She sighed in the way that twenty-somethings saddled with incompetent elders sigh. "Backcountry experience?"

"Yes."

"Here?"

"Appalachians, Blue Ridge, Smokies. Not here."

Another sigh, this one accompanied by a half eye-roll. "You at least know how to read a topo map and can navigate, right? I mean with a compass, not a damn phone."

"Yes."

"Right, then. You stick with me." One of the boys, the tall one, snickered and elbowed his buddy, who seemed heartbroken that he hadn't been assigned to partner with Ginny. "What we're doing is a hasty search. Basically we're clearing our assigned sectors of any obvious places where a person wanting to be found could be, and looking for any signs that Bill could have come through there—so be careful on the trail that you look before you step; we don't want to disturb any tracks. We move fast, so stay in sight of your partner at all times and within voice distance of the rest of the team. Always." She searched out each of their faces to make sure they understood. "We shout out for Bill and then we're quiet. We listen. We look for movement. He might be hurt and lying someplace we can't see, so no chitchat. Listen. Watch. Move on. Got it?"

"What if we clear our area but miss him, and he's actually there?" Nick asked, regretting how old and pessimistic he sounded. No, actually he sounded like Lucy, always preparing for the worst.

"That's why this is called a hasty search. We're gathering any evidence we can to bring back to the team leaders so they can prioritize where to spend manpower on a more thorough search." She jerked her chin at Nick. "I know you're a friend of Sheriff Beachey's, but trust me, we know what we're doing. Even those two clowns." She frowned at the two boys, who were half turned away, giggling at some private joke.

Ginny gave Nick a map and pointed. "Here's where we are. We'll head off the road here to our first quadrant."

Nick stumbled down the road behind her, studying the map. At least some of the land appeared relatively flat—a meadow alongside a stream at the bottom of a valley. But all the land on either side was indicated by stacks of topo lines, meaning steep going up and even steeper coming down. Why would Bill ever have headed into such extreme wilderness without letting anyone know? He was an experienced outdoorsman; he knew better than that.

"This search area, it's based on the location his last message was sent from?" he asked Amy, catching up to her.

"We've narrowed things as much as we could based off how far they estimated he was from the cell tower in Elk City. It's still a big country, and with only the one tower to ping from, there's nothing to triangulate with to limit our search area." She gestured with her chin and stopped to let the boys catch up. On the north side of the road, the land rose gradually. Trees crowded together as they fought for light. But on the south side, there was a clearing—or rather a cliff. A sheer drop of maybe a hundred feet leading down to the creek he'd seen on the map. Sharp granite jags of rock surrounded by breathtakingly stunning red, blue, and purple flowers covered the base of the cliff.

"Fireweed," Ginny told him. "And paintbrush and lupine." She pointed to the flat stretch of meadow on the other side of the stream, then beyond it to the rugged wall of the other side of the canyon and the heavily forested peaks beyond. "We aim to clear all this before nightfall."

Nick sucked in his breath and gripped

Lucy's walking stick tightly, taken aback not just by the beauty but also the challenge. He could understand the allure of getting lost in such overwhelming, pristine wilderness. Everything was sharper, every step fraught with danger and the anticipation of what wonder might be found around the next bend. Everything was clearer. Was that what Bill was searching for—clarity?

He remembered the text, and his heart grew heavy. Bill's words didn't sound like a man eager for enlightenment. They sounded like a man who'd given up hope.

Chapter 13

Lucy said goodbye to Nick and climbed back into Judith's van. Soon the staging area was vanishing into a cloud of dust behind them as the van rattled back down the dirt road. Since the staging grounds were on the far western edge of the search area, they were the only people going in this direction; everyone else was headed farther into the wilderness, traveling east, north, or south.

They were maybe halfway back to town when Judith turned up a narrow gravel and dirt lane that led through a stand of beech before winding its way up the mountain. The ascent was gradual, passing meadows that opened out onto southern or western-facing vistas then returning to the thick cover of the trees, a variety of evergreens interspersed with oak and aspen.

But what struck Lucy was how quiet it was. So peaceful. Growing up, their tiny home near the top of a mountain in the Alleghenies had never felt like this—as a kid, she was always thrilling to the next discovery and adventure that the forest brought. What she sensed was probably due to the difference in her age. Now she was old enough to simply lean her elbow out the open window and bask in the light and the sweet scent that changed subtly with every curve they rounded.

"How long have you lived here?" she asked Judith.

"Going on ten years now," the older woman answered. "But if I live here another ten, I'll still be considered a newcomer."

"Have you been coroner all that time?"

"For the past eight years. It's one of those jobs no one really wants—the pay won't even cover your gas, the hours are definitely not convenient, and there's no budget, so you have to get creative with what tests you run. Guy before me was a EMT, but he joined the Army and left, so Judge Carson asked me—and here I am."

"Is it hard? I mean, since you're not a medical doctor?"

"At first I was worried I'd miss something. I bought a whole slew of reference books and subscribed to all the journals. But turns out what kills people is a whole lot like what kills animals. Doing stupid shit, eating stupid shit, fighting over stupid shit. Kinda ironic, if you ask me."

Lucy glanced at Judith, taken aback by her vulgarity. But then she realized that the other woman was finally letting her guard down and relaxing. "Guess we're not as evolved as we'd like to think."

"I'm sure you figured that out pretty fast with the cases you handled with the FBI. Bill said you caught serial killers and child predators." Judith's face wrinkled with disgust. "We have our share of trouble up here—too much drinking, not enough work to pay the bills—but nothing like that." They rounded one last curve, a sweeping meadow of wild flowers below them and a large log cabin with a wide veranda coming in sight at the end of the drive. There were more flowers lining the front walk—native wild flowers interspersed with cultivated plants like hydrangea and floribunda roses. Vines of sweet pea released a heavenly scent as they curled up the porch columns.

Judith and Lucy climbed out of the van, Lucy clutching her now useless daypack, feeling awkward and hesitant. A woman appeared at the screen door, peered out at them, then vanished. About the same age as Deena and same dark hair—her sister?

Judith didn't hesitate. She bounded up the steps and through the screen door, almost as if she owned the place. Lucy wondered about that, but then Deena appeared from the far side of the veranda, a shawl wrapped tight around her despite the heat. "Lucy, you're here."

Deena was fifteen years older than Lucy but somehow always managed to appear younger with her long, dark hair, ballerina-straight carriage, and the way her face was always in motion, expressing emotion and interest in everything. But not now. Now her face revealed every moment of her fifty-five years, her shoulders slumped with fatigue and worry. Lucy dropped her pack to the porch floor and rushed to her friend, pulling her into a hug.

"I'm so glad you came," Deena finally said as they separated. She shed no tears, yet her voice sounded as if she'd been crying. "If anyone can find him, it's you."

Lucy had no idea what to say to that—after all, she wasn't out searching for Bill, unlike Nick. "I'm so sorry—" she started.

Deena cut her off with a wave of her shawl. "No. I've had enough babying and mothering and awkward platitudes from everyone else. They're doing the best they can, and if he's just lost in the woods, they'll find him. But," she eyed Lucy, "you said he called you. Three times."

"Yes, something about a cold case? Or an old case? Wait. Here." Lucy grabbed her phone and replayed the voicemails for Deena.

Deena held the phone in both her hands, cradling it. Then she played the messages a second time. "He sounds so excited. When you first told me it was about an old case, I thought it was something back in Denver. He had one go wrong recently. In fact—" She shook her head, waving off her own words as if they trespassed into a forbidden area. "I wonder if this is anything to do with..." She turned and Lucy followed her around to the side of the house.

The cabin was built with its main door facing west, the north side backed up to the side of the mountain, so Lucy had missed its main feature until Deena led her around to the house's southern exposure. Here the deck was open and wider, circling all the way across to the eastern wall to make the most of the stunning scenery. The windows climbed from floor to roof, revealing an open-ceilinged great room inside. "Deena, this is gorgeous."

"Bill's dad built it back when he came home from the Second World War. Took him almost a decade, but he refused to propose to his girl until he had a home worthy of her. Bill was born a year after they married, but then his mom died less than a year after that—rheumatic fever. They could have been together so much longer... his dad never got over that. He was such a sad and angry man."

Deena leaned over the railing her gaze searching the horizon. "Bill had a love-hate relationship with both this place and his dad. He loved his work in the city, but after his dad died and we began to think about coming back here to live, when we finally did, it was like a weight was lifted. I swear you wouldn't recognize him, Lucy. He lost ten pounds just from being outside, walking. He's off his blood pressure meds; doesn't need them anymore. And yet, sometimes, there's still this shadow, like he's looked in the mirror and sees his father looking back. Winter was bad, but once the sun came back and the snow left, he was back to his old self. But I never heard him excited, not about work, not until those messages."

"Was he working on anything special? Something to do with a cold case?"

A strange half-chuckle shook Deena.

"Come inside, see for yourself."

She opened one of the sliding doors, and they stepped inside. A river rock fireplace took up most of the wall to Lucy's left, while to her right was a door leading to another room where the hum of a vacuum could be heard. The kitchen was in the rear of the house, as was the dining room, its Shaker-style table strewn with maps. A radio base station crowded in with candle holders and family photos on the buffet behind it. Judith and Deena's sister were sitting there, holding cups of steaming tea and making notes on the maps as they listened to the searchers' chatter.

The floor was heart of pine topped with thick colorful wool rugs; the furniture simple, arranged to face the windows and the vista they displayed. Deena led Lucy to the staircase that rose between the kitchen and dining room, which opened onto a loft and another closed door to a room over the kitchen. With its two large computer monitors and whiteboards covered with sketches, the loft clearly functioned as Deena's office—she was a graphic designer specializing in logos and branding. Now she paused outside the closed door as if she wanted to knock. But then she opened it.

"Welcome to Bill's world of wackiness." Deena stepped aside to let Lucy in. The room was maybe twelve by twelve with a single window covered with newspaper. No, not newspaper—newspaper clippings, haphazardly stuck on by pieces of tape, their tails flapping and shimmying in the breeze of the ceiling fan. One wall acted as a whiteboard for Bill's notes scrawled in a rainbow of colors, arrows arcing back and forth, a time line of dates across the top, items circled with question marks and stars.

The other two walls held more paper—thumbtacked police reports, printouts of lab results and witness statements, along with a kaleidoscope of sticky notes. In one corner was a desk with an empty area that clearly once held the radio base station that had been moved downstairs. Other than that, the room was empty. No chairs, no knickknacks, none of the official accoutrements that thirty years of law enforcement leaves behind.

"Before he became sheriff, he spent his time hiking, exploring... He was fascinated with an old legend about a cache of hidden gold. But then, after he took the job... all this started."

Lucy circled the room, following a well-worn path in the carpeting that no amount of vacuuming could erase. Bill's footsteps, pacing, stalking...what? She glanced at the dates and headlines. Deaths. Going back a decade. All local. None suspicious.

"I don't understand. What was he looking for?"

Deena shrugged. "Patterns, questions. At first it was just boredom combined with wanting to familiarize himself with the department's history. So he started talking with the old timers—not just Sheriff Langer, he's moved to Florida, but Harriet the dispatcher, who pretty much runs things, Gus Holmstead, folks like him who have lived here forever. But then things changed. Bill became...obsessed."

Lucy nodded. The word fit—and felt familiar. She often plunged into cases the same way. Even Nick sometimes didn't understand; from the outside it could look a bit manic and out of control. "He saw something. A pattern, something that made him call me." She stopped in front of the empty desk. There was a dust pattern for other more than the radio. "Did he have a laptop?"

"He took it with him. I don't know if he left it at the office or had it with him in the Jeep." Deena turned in a circle and then focused on Lucy once more, her expression anxious. "When I heard those voicemails... I haven't heard him that excited about something in a long, long time. But, Lucy...maybe it's not real. Maybe he saw something that wasn't really there, something he wanted to see because he was bored and needed a challenge?" The hope that sparked her voice when they'd been outside on the deck had vanished, replaced by resignation. "I thought maybe you'd see the same thing. Tell me he wasn't..."

Lucy said nothing, trying to follow Bill's mental trail. "Give me a little time."

Deena nodded, her shoulders sagging

once more. She crept backwards out the door.

"Deena," Lucy called after her. She'd seen rooms like this before—including her own offices, both at the FBI and Beacon Falls, in fact.

"Yes?"

"I have no idea if he was right or not—and I may be wrong. But I think Bill thought, he was trying to see—" She stopped herself, not wanting to give Deena false hope. Plus, the idea was outlandish. But Deena turned to her, eyes gleaming, begging for a lifeline.

Lucy hauled in a breath. "I think maybe he was trying, that he may have found, or thought he found... a serial killer."

Chapter 14

The first time Bill woke, it was night. He'd been shivering, nauseated, clammy with sweat, and afraid if he ever closed his eyes again, he might not see the light of day. So he sat and tried to keep his breathing steady, concentrating on his core muscles to conserve heat. During the night, he spotted the lights of planes flying low and heard the rumble of helicopters several times, but none came close.

He remembered the climber out in Utah who'd fallen, gotten trapped by a rock, and ended up cutting off his own hand. Or was it a leg? At the time Bill had thought, *What a damn fool.* But now who was the fool? No one knew where he was because he'd decided to find a nice place to pick huckleberries and surprise his wife with a picnic. If he died, Deena would never forgive him.

So he decided not to die.

You can live three minutes without air, three days without water, three weeks without food, his grandfather had told him during one of their hunting trips. *But most important thing you need to know about survival is it's all in the mind. You gotta be stubborn, certain you're gonna make it out alive. You lose that will to survive, you're a goner for sure.*

That trip, Bill had been nine. They'd visited the site where Lloyd Magruder was killed. Magruder had been beaten, hung, thrown off a cliff, then his body burned. Alive, some said, taking pride in how hard it was to kill a Magruder.

But he was still dead. And even though there were monuments to the Magruder name all over the state of Idaho, it had been a Beachey who'd tracked down those three outlaws, all the way to San Francisco, and brought them to justice. That was the kind of stubborn that ran in the Beachey blood, his grandfather reminded him when they bedded down for the night. When Bill woke the next morning, his grandfather was gone, and so were their horses and all their supplies.

At first he'd been shocked by the cruelty of the test. But by the time he'd made it back home three days later, the look of pride on both his father and grandfather more than made up for a few nights being cold and the bug bites and blisters. Beacheys never quit. That wasn't the family motto because it didn't need to be said out loud or embroidered on any pillow. It was just in their blood.

The sun finally rose, and Bill was still there. His head still throbbed and his mind felt like it was smothering in a thick fog, but he fought through the muddle and assessed his situation. At the very least he had a concussion, but when he gingerly touched the cut on his head he felt a divot there like the bone had been staved in. So more than a concussion—a skull fracture. Best he stayed sitting up, hopefully keeping any swelling down.

Moving down, he definitely had a broken cheekbone, and his eye was still swollen shut. His neck was fine, thank God. A few cracked ribs on both sides, but he could breathe okay as long as he kept it slow and steady, no deep breaths. His belly worried him—it hurt a bit on the left, but mostly up under his ribs, so maybe it was nothing. He made a makeshift sling for his broken right arm by unbuttoning his second and third shirt buttons and sliding his arm across his body and inside his shirt. It wouldn't hold if he moved much, but just sitting there it worked fine.

The bleeding on his leg had stopped and didn't restart when he loosened his belt. He kept the belt there just in case—it was too much trouble to take it off anyways. The other leg, the one so twisted he got nauseated every time he looked at it... well, there just was no way he could do anything about it, so he stopped looking at it.

The cliff faced east out over the canyon, but the narrow crevice he'd landed in, between the cliff's southern wall and a large boulder, was shielded from the sun except for a stream of light that crept up his legs to mid-thigh. Thankfully the rocks absorbed enough heat that he didn't think hypothermia would be an issue—but it also meant no search planes would ever spot him.

He toyed with the idea of dragging himself farther out onto the ledge, but it fell off sharply, and he wasn't sure how stable the terrain was. Still, he had almost psyched himself to do it when a glint of reflected sunlight caught his eye. It came from behind him to the left, deeper back into the crevice behind the boulder. A protected patch where the sun never hit directly, so there was a puddle of water left over from the rain two nights ago.

Water. He lowered himself onto his left side and used his good arm to drag himself to the puddle. Pain shrieked through his body as his legs protested but he ignored it, focusing on the elixir of life. He needed the water to live; everything else could go to hell.

He reached the puddle, dipped his lips to the chilled water, and lapped it into his mouth like a beast.

When he'd drunk his fill, he sat up, leaning against the cliff wall, not even realizing that a crooked smile had twisted his lips. He had shelter, he had water, he had the Beachey mule-stubborn willfulness in his blood.

He was going to live.

CHAPTER 15

LUCY HAD DINNER WITH DEENA and her family—a delicious meal prepared by Deena's mother but punctuated with such uncomfortable silences that Lucy fled as soon as they finished cleaning up. Deena had given her the keys to Bill's truck so she wouldn't be dependent on bumming rides from Judith.

When she arrived back at the motel, she begged off the festivities Judith and her staff were preparing to bolster the search volunteers' morale and instead reviewed her notes on Bill's cold cases in her room while she waited for Nick. A few of the cases were intriguing, others seemed highly unlikely, but she forwarded the info to Wash, her tech analyst back at Beacon

Falls, in the hopes that he could find a pattern or lead for her to follow.

It was almost ten o'clock when Nick finally stumbled in, sunburned, bug bit, and exhausted. He flopped on the bed, too tired to even shower, eyes half closed as he listened to what she'd found at Bill's home.

"Wait." He opened one eye when she finished. "You told Deena you agreed with Bill? That there's evidence of a serial killer?"

"I never said evidence. I said his theory had some merit."

Nick sat up. "A bunch of old newspaper clippings aren't evidence of anything. Lucy, how could you be so irresponsible? To let Deena—"

"What's the problem? I simply gave her one more possible explanation for Bill's disappearance."

"Two more, actually. Either he's chasing after a serial killer without letting anyone know—and we both know Bill's not stupid or reckless—or he's fallen victim to some deranged killer."

"She's already worried about him lying

dead at the bottom of a ravine somewhere," Lucy argued. "At least if he really is out there with a killer, the killer has reason to keep him alive long enough to find out what Bill knows and who he's told. That would explain the weird text to Judy."

"Right. I'm sure imagining Bill in the hands of a killer will let her sleep soundly tonight." Nick bounced to his feet and swung the curtain hard as he strode into the alcove with the sink and vanity. He washed his face, brushed his teeth—all done so loudly and with abrupt motions that she knew he was seriously pissed off.

"You always do this," he said after rinsing and spitting. "Your imagination works overtime finding the worst possible scenario."

She wanted to argue that she was usually right but knew that wasn't really his point. "At least you can't blame my job this time," she sniped back.

"I don't blame your job—"

"Sure you do. You and Megan both. Don't think I don't see it." She turned away, rubbing her eyes with the heels of her hands. "I'm just so tired."

Nick rejoined her on the bed and wrapped an arm around her. "Maybe you blame your job and just can't admit it. There are other jobs out there, you know. A ton of other jobs you'd be brilliant at."

But would they give her what she needed? The adrenaline rush of chasing a killer, the satisfaction of saving a victim, the thrill of knowing that if only for a few moments she had the power to tip the scales of justice back into balance... Except lately it seemed those moments were getting shorter and more fleeting. Lately it felt like no one really cared about justice at all, as if it had become an outdated concept replaced by return on investment and success rates and plea bargains. Exactly why her passion for victims and pursuing their truth had gotten her kicked out of the FBI.

Things were definitely better at Beacon Falls, but still, she ended up leaving her family to work cases, always worried about them while they worried about her. Somehow they always paid the price for her doing her job.

"So are we okay?" Nick asked after a long moment.

"We?" His abrupt change of topic caught her off guard. Or maybe not so abrupt—they'd been tiptoeing past the issue for months. Or in Lucy's case, a flat out dash to avoid it.

"I mean, it's been an eventful year. And we don't really talk about it too much. Should we be?"

Translation: Lucy refused to talk about what happened in January. Being kidnapped by a sadistic killer, mauled by his vicious attack dog, facing him as he threatened to kill Nick and Megan, and finally learning that he'd murdered Lucy's mother. One night, eight months ago, yet she still relived it every day, and the memories stripped her psyche as raw as the constant pain her damaged leg brought.

So, no. She really didn't want to reveal her struggles to Nick. She knew he wanted—needed—to help; it was who he was. But the thought of it was overwhelming. The guilt; the sense of absolute, abysmal failure. What she'd done that night, what had happened because of her...she could never forgive herself.

"I'm worried," he continued. "I thought leaving the FBI, getting this new job, would be good for you. For us. But you seem to be using your new job as an excuse to never come home—you're always on the road."

She waved her hand in a dismissal, the shadow she cast swooping over the wall behind Nick like an eagle diving for prey. "I go where the cases take me. I can't just sit at a desk all day and let everyone else do the heavy lifting."

Like she had today. She turned her back to him, bent over to yank off her boots, then sighed in relief as she removed the splint from her left ankle. It kept the pain of walking at bay and saved her foot from constant scraping against the ground she couldn't feel beneath it, but there was nothing like the freedom of having it off.

"Okay, so maybe the problem isn't your job. I still feel like you're pushing me away, avoiding talking about what's going on."

She stood, her back still to him, jerking her shirt over her head, quickly changing into the tee and shorts she slept in. "And exactly what do you think is going on?"

"I don't know." He finished changing, threw his dirty clothes at his suitcase and missed but didn't bother picking them up off the floor—a definite warning that he was even more upset than she'd realized. "Maybe you can tell me. Starting with why, when I called home to check our messages, there was a call from the surgeon's office wanting to talk to you about pre-authorization for your operation."

Shit. She'd almost forgotten about the surgeon—or more truthfully, she'd successfully avoided thinking about the surgeon and his plans for her leg. Nick came up behind her and placed his palms on her shoulders. "Lucy. What operation? What's going on?"

Her shoulders heaved as she blew her breath out, his hands slipping away from her body. She walked past him and stretched out on top of the bed covers, reaching for the special moisturizer she used on her scars every night.

"They want to amputate. The say my bones are old, so it's better to do it now than wait, that they've done everything they can for the pain."

"Lord knows you've done all you can. Your progress and your dedication to your rehab have been incredible. If this is the best way to alleviate your pain and increase function—"

"Yeah, yeah, yeah." She rubbed the cream a bit too vigorously, unleashing an electrical shock of pain when she pressed against one of the screws in her tibia. "That's what the doctor said, too. Although, by the way, I'm not even sure he's old enough to shave."

Nick eased under the covers, encroaching onto her side of the bed. "You don't like giving up. Not on anybody—or anything."

Sometimes she hated how sensible he could be. Being forced out of the FBI after working so hard to return was bad enough, but now all that was for nothing? They were right back where they'd started eight months ago when the dog had mauled her. That awful first night they'd almost amputated—she'd been unconscious, in shock—but Nick had persuaded the surgeons to try to save her leg. She almost felt guiltier about wasting the chance he'd given her than the thought of losing her leg.

Nick understood without her saying a word. Sometimes she hated how easily he could read her, but most of the time it was one of her favorite things about him. "You're not a failure, Lucy."

They sat in silence for a moment until Lucy finally finished her attack on her ankle, put the cream away, and slid under the sheets already warm from his body heat.

"If you don't want to talk to me, I get it. Have you talked to Dr. Cranston?" Cranston was her trauma counselor—past tense.

Lucy looked away. "Haven't seen her in a while."

He slumped back, rattling the headboard against the wall. "People come to you for help all the time. Why is it so hard for you to ask for help when you need it? Are you worried it's a sign of weakness? Or that people will take advantage? Not respect you?" He paused, searching her face. "Or that no one will come if you ask?"

She flinched.

"Lucy." He wrapped an arm around her shoulders and pulled her to him. "Do you really think if the situation was reversed, if you were the one who needed help, that no one would come? All those people at your party last night—they love you. Any one of them would drop everything if you called and needed them."

She shrugged, her face moving against his shoulder.

"Is it the thought of the amputation, then? I know plenty of guys at the VA who'd love to have had a say before they woke up to find a limb missing. And with the new prosthetics—"

She pulled back to her side of the bed, arranging her pillows as an excuse not to answer. The light was behind her, sending her shadow out across the space between them, casting Nick in darkness.

"With a prosthetic and rehab, you'd be pretty much back to full capability," he continued. Then he paused, thinking. "But that would give you no excuse when people ask you why you left the FBI."

Her pension wasn't technically medical disability; rather, it came from a line of duty injury fund that the new director had discretion over. One more thing for Lucy to feel guilty about: taking money for a full pension when she hadn't put in her full thirty years. Not that the powers that be had given her any choice in the matter, which of course also rankled. Every time she opened the check from them, she felt so...useless. Powerless. Basically just *less*. Less than who she once had been. Who she wanted to be.

And now they wanted to cut away part of her body.

Nick moved abruptly, his head knocking against the wall. "Or, wait—you don't want to try to go back, do you? Fight them, try to get your old job back at the FBI?"

"My old job no longer exists, remember?" she said bitterly. "There's nothing left for me there."

He ignored the warning in her voice.

"Maybe. But all this stuff that's happened—it's eating you up. And it didn't just happen to you. It happened to us."

"Us?" Two thousand miles away from home in a strange place, on a strange bed, surrounded by strangers, and he chose now to fix everything wrong with them? With her?

"I just want you to know. You're not alone in all this."

Ahh...that explained his sudden insistence. If they couldn't find Bill, if he was dead, then Deena was alone to struggle through the pain. Lucy thought about that. She understood what Nick was saying, but she didn't like it. Not at all. If bad things were going to happen, she wanted them to happen only to her—never to him or Megan. She *wanted* to be in it alone.

But that wasn't Nick. A man of faith—in both science and religion—he believed in healing, thought there was always an answer if they just worked through things together.

"Do you believe in karma?" she asked, looking past him at their shadows on the wall.

"You forget. I know your greatest fear." His voice dropped into a whisper, but his words were what shook her.

"Can we not talk about this now?" She purposefully let her frustration bleed into her tone.

Once again he ignored her warning. "More magical thinking. Say it aloud and it might come true. You know that's not how the universe works."

"It's how my mind works."

"I know. But I can see you, caught in this cycle, this churning. And refusing to talk about it is only making things worse."

He had a point. It definitely wasn't making things better—just like her sessions with the trauma counselor hadn't—but neither was this conversation.

"It's me. And Megan." He jutted his chin in defiance.

She fought a flinch. And for the first time ever, dared to say the words. "Losing either of you—I couldn't survive that."

"People do."

"I'm not as strong as you think I am." She shifted her leg, and her ankle protested with a shriek of pain. Nick sensed it and curled into her body, sharing his warmth, a gesture that used to be as welcoming as coming home, his touch a sanctuary that the cruel humanity she faced on a daily basis could never breach.

At least that's what she believed and trusted in. Nick was where she'd placed her faith. Once upon a time.

Lucy turned away from his invitation and reached for the light, casting them into darkness and banishing the shadows.

Chapter 16

THE NEXT MORNING, Lucy left a note for Nick while he was taking his shower, grabbed her pack, maps, and phone, and then took Bill's truck down the hill and into town. The sun had barely nudged a thin crescent over the mountains to the east, but she felt wide-awake and anxious to get going. The thought of joining the search volunteers at breakfast in the main lodge made her teeth ache—and she was still unsettled by her not-quite-argument definitely-not-therapy-session with Nick last night. It drove her nuts when he tried to psych their relationship and he damn well knew it, which meant he must be pretty upset to have started down that road at all.

That didn't mean it helped. Didn't mean she wanted to continue the conversation, dissecting everything wrong with her psyche. And sure as hell didn't mean she was in any mood to watch him ride off with the search team while she stayed behind.

She grabbed a quick protein and fat laden breakfast at the café in town and drove out of town along the Magruder Corridor to the turnoff for the Holmstead ranch—the last place Bill was seen—and parked. She climbed up to the truck's dusty hood and scrutinized her map as she sipped her coffee. She circled the search territory, then marked the cell tower in Elk City and drew a ring at around twenty miles, a reasonable estimate of how far a tower's reception could carry, and then another ring at forty miles, the outermost limit. A large swath of green dotted by amoeboid white blobs covered the intersection, a Venn diagram drawn by Salvador Dali.

A hell of a lot of ground to cover. But if Bill were inside the search radius—and wanted to be found—and if he could move at all or call out, he would have been found by now. That was where the SAR teams had gone wrong, she was certain. Because if Bill wanted to be found, why would he have spent almost twenty-four hours away from home without contacting anyone? And why send that cryptic text when he finally did make contact? To Judith, of all people.

No, he either did not want to be found or was in a position where he didn't want civilians looking for him. Which meant the searchers were looking in the wrong place. But what was the right direction?

Her phone rang. "Hi, Megan. How's it going?"

"Grandma said to call to ask if it's okay if we go camping. It means I won't be able to call again until Monday."

"Do you want to go?" When she was a little girl, Megan had loved camping—the more primitive the better, to the point where she preferred to sleep outside without a tent if the weather was nice. But then she turned into a pre-teen and a teenager, and now it was a struggle just to get her to go on a day hike if it meant leaving her cell phone behind.

"Yeah. Dad sent me pictures of where you guys are, and it looks cool. Grandpa said there are places like that near here, so he's taking me to his favorite spot where he took Dad when Dad was a kid."

"Are you going to be in a tent? You know that means sleeping on the ground, right? And no electricity?"

"Grandma and Grandpa are coming," she said, implying that if two old people could do it, so could she. "Please, is it okay?"

Lucy had to admit she had grown accustomed to having Megan tethered to the safety line that was her cell phone. But she also hated that Megan might miss out on the world beyond a six-inch screen. "Yes, it's fine. But text or call as soon as you get back. And listen to your grandparents. Take it easy on them, okay? No complaining, even if you don't like it."

"Mom—" She drew it out to two syllables of teen angst.

"Love you. Have fun."

“Thanks, bye.”

Her team back at Beacon Falls were three hours ahead in their work day, so she took advantage of the cell reception and called them. Wash would be on his second cup of coffee at least, so at his peak energy level.

“Hey boss,” he answered. “How’s the wild, wild west? Your friend okay?”

“I don’t think so.” She filled him in on what had happened. “Can you check the cell tower, see if there’s some way to narrow the direction or distance?”

“How accurate’s your timeline? That text might not have been sent when it said it was.”

“But it was time stamped—”

He snorted. “Have I taught you nothing? Anything can be spoofed. Easy as pie to schedule something for when you want it sent or who it appears to have been sent from, especially a text.”

Her phone dinged with a text from Megan, but when she glanced at it, it read: *SEE WHAT I MEAN? NOT SENT BY MEGAN OR HER PHONE.* Followed by a goofy set of emojis.

"Okay, you made your point. So if I can't rely on the text or the time frame, what can I work with? How about the three calls he made to me?"

"Yeah, let me dig in to those." Since her phone was a work phone, he already had access to its records. "Can you forward me the info the police there got from your friend's phone? Or better yet, get me permission to talk with the cell company? Whoever owns that tower."

"The state police handled it, but Deena gave us permission to access Bill's account data. I'll forward you the email with all the contact info and her authorization. Remind them this is a critical missing person case involving a law enforcement officer; they shouldn't give you any trouble."

"Don't worry, I'll get it one way or another. So where you're calling me now, how far is that from the tower?"

"Not sure. I only have one bar, though." She glanced at the map. "About twenty-eight miles. But I'm also getting a few bars on my Wi-Fi—does that make a difference?"

"Yes, if his phone was set up to piggyback Wi-Fi and cellular. Probably was—anything to boost a signal out there, right? Where is the Wi-Fi coming from?"

"I don't know for sure, but there's a ranch a few miles from here. They have a guest lodge, and their website said they have Wi-Fi."

"Probably satellite. Maybe with extenders or repeaters? Let me play with this and get back to you." He sounded distracted, as if she'd given him a puzzle box to unlock. "How do people talk to each other out there? I just pulled up the map, and you're like in the middle of nowhere."

"The most remote area of the lower forty-eight. The locals take that as a point of pride."

"Yeah, but police covering all that, not to mention the search parties—"

"Radios. They all have radios. Even Bill's home has a base station. Deena said he took calls from there. And I've seen a few folks with sat phones." Like what Judith and those geologic engineers who'd hitched a ride with them yesterday carried.

"I got your email with those old cases," Wash continued. "Nothing interesting yet, but I'll keep looking."

"Thanks. Maybe do background checks on anyone that pops out at you?" She glanced over her shoulder at the sound of a vehicle approaching. "Gotta go. Text me if you find anything."

"So you're staying in one place where I can actually reach you?"

"No, but I'll be checking in with Deena." She gave him Deena's landline number. "You can call her if it's urgent."

"What about Nick?"

"He's out searching."

A forest service truck pulled up beside her, Gleason at the wheel. The road was barely wide enough to accommodate both trucks even though she'd parked at the far edge.

"Bye, thanks." She hung up.

Gleason slid out from behind the wheel over to the passenger window and rolled it down. "You lost?"

"No, I was headed over to the Holmstead

ranch. I wanted to see if they remembered anything, but then I was afraid maybe it was too early."

He glanced at the sun cresting over the mountains. "Not for Amy and Gus. They'll have been up for hours—got livestock to tend to. I'm headed that way myself. A bear trap needs fresh bait. Want a ride? I can introduce you. Gus gets a bit ornery around strangers."

"Sounds like a plan." She grabbed her map and pack and hopped into his truck. "Shouldn't you be out coordinating the search?"

"The District Ranger came in from Darby, and is taking over. And someone's got to take care of business."

Lucy wondered if the District Ranger was there because a sheriff missing for two days was bound to attract media attention or because he thought Gleason hadn't done a good job with the search. "Why do you have a bear trap on private land? Wouldn't you want to keep the bears away from their livestock?"

"Exactly. The Holmstead spread includes a lot more than just grazing land. Most of it is just as much wilderness as the Forest Service land. And it's not like bears or wolves can read a map—they simply head to where the water and food is."

"Wolves?"

"Yes ma'am. They're smarter than your average bear, too." She smiled at his cartoon reference, then realized he was serious—and probably too young to even know who Yogi Bear was. Which made her feel even older.

They slowed and turned off the main drive leading to the ranch and onto a more rugged track heading into the woods. He stopped the truck in a small clearing at the base of a tiny waterfall that cascaded down to create a creek bed. Across the water was a boulder field climbing up the side of a hill, while to their right a timber fall acted as a dam. The area in front of it was teeming with sumac, wild flowers, and small bushes with dark blue berries. Nestled in them sat a ten-foot steel cylinder on a trailer with a heavy door raised in the air by a hoist. The bear trap. It looked a lot more sophisticated than the simple culvert traps she'd seen back in Pennsylvania.

Gleason turned the truck around—it took a five-point turn, given the trees and bushes—and parked. "Here." He handed her a laptop and opened a video file. "You watch this while I check for scat and tracks. Don't get out until I give the all clear."

At first Lucy bristled, feeling like a child being given a toy to distract her and make her stay put. But Gleason was a professional, and he was doing her a favor, plus the video...fascinating. It was from a trail camera aimed at a similar culvert trap. It must have been motion-activated, judging from the choppiness—but the animals that had activated it weren't the bears the trap and its bait were meant to entice, but rather a lone wolf creeping into position near the trap's open door.

Like the trap here, this one lay in a canyon near a creek bed. The wolf easily concealed itself among the bushes at the edge of the stream—if the camera hadn't caught it, Lucy never would have been able to track it. The footage stuttered and then began again as a large black bear ambled past, stopping almost in front of the camera. It raised its head, sniffed, circled, almost started back away from the trap but then stopped and sniffed again, shaking its snout as if torn. Then it shuffled a few steps toward the trap—and the wolf waiting in ambush—before stopping again.

Lucy rewound the video and focused on the hillside behind the bear. She zoomed in and slowed it down, the video turning grainy but still clear enough that she saw that the wolf wasn't alone. As the bear hesitated, she spotted three more wolves moving into position, outflanking the bear. She started the video at regular speed again. "Run," she urged the bear. "Can't you see it's an ambush?"

The bear rose up from four feet to two, snout in the air, sniffing again. This time it shook its entire body, made a snuffling grunt, and whirled to run back the way it came. But the wolves didn't give up so easily. The one hidden near the trap quickly gave chase, followed by the others across the creek on the ridge.

The final frame caught the silhouette of a large silver wolf alone, staring upstream. Lucy could swear it wore the same expression every field instructor she'd ever worked with had when they dissected an operation during the after-action brief, figuring out what went wrong and how to do it right next time.

For a brief moment the wolf turned and stared directly at the camera—at her. As if it knew it was being watched. It bared its teeth, eyes gleaming with anticipation. She shuddered. She'd seen that expression before—eight months ago on the face of thc dog right before it attacked her.

Next time, you're mine, it seemed to say. *Next time, you won't get away.*

Chapter 17

NICK WAS ASHAMED TO ADMIT that he was glad when he got out of the shower to find Lucy gone. He'd thought he was in great shape—he ran five days a week, did weights two, and biked on the weekends, except in the winter. But between the sitting in a cramped airplane seat for half the day and then spending the other half scrambling up and down hills, boulders, scree fields, and goat trails searching for Bill, every muscle in his body wanted nothing more than to go back to bed for another twelve hours.

Not solely his body; his spirit was equally exhausted. They'd found nothing—none of the search teams had. The sense of failure was overwhelming. Especially as he knew he should get out there, rejoin the teams—some now into their third day—and do what he could to help keep their spirits high.

But he just couldn't. Lucy leaving early gave him a way to save face, to conveniently be too late to get a ride to today's scheduled coordination session when the searchers would be given their new assignments. He slowly dressed, trying his best and failing not to scratch the bug bites that covered his arms and legs. Just because he wasn't going out into the field didn't mean he wouldn't still be contributing something to the cause. He'd go to Deena, and try his best to help her through this ordeal.

Three days of not knowing. He sank onto the bed, his socks in his hand, suddenly without the strength to put them on. Those first three days Lucy had been in the ICU, the doctors weren't sure if she'd live or die. Her injuries, the shock, fighting off infection from the dog bites... Three days he'd waited, holding her hand that lay limp in his, watching machines do the work of living and breathing, avoiding the gaze of the nurses, unable to bear it if they gave up on her.

He'd never felt so alone in his life. Powerless, all his training and knowledge futile in the face of mortality. Nothing to do except sit and wait and pray as hope surrendered to despair.

Back then he'd been too drained, exhausted in the most literal sense of the word, to help himself, much less Lucy. But now, maybe, he could offer Deena the comfort of a friend who understood what she was going through.

Finally he finished dressing, glanced at the clock to make sure the others were long gone—although the younger volunteers, a group from Lewiston and another from Boise, were rowdy and loud enough that he'd heard them leave, excited that today would be the day they would become heroes—and made his way down to the main building, going through the middle door that led to the restaurant.

There he put together a plate from the remnants left by the hordes that had gone through the buffet like a swarm of locusts and filled a mug with steaming coffee. Judith found him as he was finishing.

"Nick," she said, getting her own cup of coffee and joining him. "Need a ride out to the morning search briefing? I just got back from taking the last van load, but I don't mind."

"I thought I'd go over to see Deena. We got back so late last night, I feel bad I haven't had a chance yet."

"Lucy has Bill's truck, but I've kinda set up camp at his place—it's closer to the action than the sheriff's station. Want to ride out with me?"

"Thanks, Judith. That would be great. Just let me grab my gear." One lesson he'd learned from Lucy—always bring the basics with you when you're in the field. Even if you expect to spend the day sipping tea and enduring long awkward silences as you wait.

He left Judith, but instead of going out the way he'd come in, he strolled through the animal wing. Lucy didn't like this place—he'd noticed her brief panic attack, but they had an unwritten rule not to talk about them.

The same rule he'd tried to break last night, which had only led to a fight. No, not a fight—when he and Lucy fought, everything came out, the air was cleared, and they always ended up closer than before. What happened last night was the opposite of that. And he had no idea how to fix it. Silence hadn't helped, talking last night had only made things worse... what was left? Lucy felt farther away than ever, and he had no idea how to reach her.

The animals were making quiet noises as they paced their enclosures—except the sloth, who could have been stuffed for all the movement he made. The tiger moved stiffly, favoring one front leg as he leaned down to lap water from the artificial stream that ran through the front of his and the bear's habitats. The bear was busy scratching his back, rubbing up against a thick tree trunk covered in barbed wire.

Nick wandered over to the other side. There were two more of the large habitats, but they were empty, the water turned off, all vegetation removed, everything else scrubbed clean. Judith had said something about a circus lion dying. He pivoted to the empty aquariums that had held the snakes. They still had plates bolted along the bottom frames listing both the scientific and common names: copperhead, water moccasin, Burmese python, coral snake, death adder, green tree python, black mamba. He was surprised there were no spaces for rattlesnakes—he knew from what Ginny had said and the briefings yesterday that Idaho had several species.

He continued out to the path to his cabin, grabbed his daypack, and headed back to meet Judith in the front lobby. The grand hall was eerily silent except for the rustle of the birds overhead. How lonely it must be to live here when there were no tourists around. He imagined winter, the snow piled high, nowhere to go, no one to talk to... The old hotel reminded him of the one from *The Shining*. Not in architectural details, but it shared that same pervasive sense of emptiness.

Judith came bustling out of her apartment

behind the reception desk, carrying her own pack. "We'll take my work truck instead of the van, just in case I get called out on an emergency."

She led him to a white Excursion with *JK ANIMAL CARE* emblazoned on the side. He climbed into the passenger seat of the oversized SUV and craned his neck to look in the back. The cargo space had been outfitted as a mini-animal clinic, with gear packed behind glass cabinets and in storage cubbies. It reminded him of an ambulance. Everything was shiny and clean, spotless, even the tall rubber boots and extra-long black rubber gauntlets hanging from a rack beside a collection of cattle prods of various sizes.

"Quite an operation."

"Thanks. Folks around here used to take care of their own livestock and pets, but our population is trending older as more and more younger people move away. A lot of these folks take better care of their animals than they do themselves."

"So, you probably hear and see a lot. Any

thoughts on what happened to Bill?"

She was silent as they neared the end of the paved road and turned onto a hard-packed dirt road that snaked up the mountain. "I'm not sure," she finally answered. "I think maybe you might want to ask Deena."

Nick watched Judith, the way her hands easily took control of the wheel even around the steep switchbacks. Everyone out here seemed the same: in control, self-contained, ready to take on the world alone. Pioneering spirit hard at work. But Judith was in her mid-to-late fifties and she was one of the youngest full-time residents he'd met. If the younger generations kept drifting away for softer, easier lives, how much longer could that independent spirit be kept alive?

They reached Bill and Deena's home. Bill had shared photos before, and Nick knew it had been in Bill's family for several generations, but he wasn't prepared for the majestic beauty that surrounded the large log cabin with its tall windows. Breathtaking was the only adjective he could think of. Despite the lack of urban conveniences and the harsh winters, he could understand why Bill had been so excited to return home.

Deena spotted them from where she was standing on the deck, silhouetted by the early morning sun like a whaler's wife watching from her widow's walk, waiting for her husband to return. She was dressed in jeans and a loose-fitting tee, her hair pulled back in a ponytail, and a quiet air of grace surrounded her. She raced down the steps and ran to Nick, hugging him hard. "I'm so glad to see you," she told him. Then she nodded to Judith. "Go on in, Mom has coffee on."

Judith smiled, touched Deena's arm, and walked up the stairs to the front door.

"Can we walk?" Deena asked Nick. "I feel like I can't breathe in there. Everyone's so careful around me, like I'm going to break. Do I look like I'm going to break?"

"No. You don't. You look like you're...ready?" He didn't want to make assumptions, so he let his voice drift up in a question.

She hauled in a breath and guided him onto a path that hugged the side of the mountain and looked out over the valley below. "I think I am. Is that strange? Am I giving up too soon? Lucy would say I am—you know her, she never gives up on anything. You should have seen her yesterday, diving into his case notes like they were the Rosetta Stone. But," another deep breath, "I woke up this morning and this quiet certainty just settled over me. It's kind of scary but kind of soothing at the same time. Does that make sense?"

"Yes." They walked through a stand of beech and aspen that opened up onto a small meadow filled with wildflowers. "And I don't think it's giving up. Maybe more like acceptance."

"Acceptance." She tried the word on for size. Then bit her lip, nodding. "Maybe also forgiveness?"

"For yourself or Bill?"

"Both." She took both his hands and turned to face him. "Nick, I think I know what he was trying to say in that text he sent Judith. I saw it a little this winter; I thought it was a combination of no sunlight and cabin fever—in Denver the winters weren't as bad, and he had work to keep him steady. I thought he was better once he took over as sheriff and had a mission, a purpose. But...now I'm not so sure."

"Are you saying Bill was depressed?"

"Maybe. I think. But then he seemed better, happy all summer. But there was this case he worked back in Denver, and last week, it was supposed to finally go to court. He was even getting ready to fly back and testify, but..." She dropped his hand and swallowed hard. "It was a kid. Her uncle had been abusing her for years—gave her to his friends to pay off gambling debts. Until finally she told. They took the case as far as they could despite there being no DNA or slam dunk evidence, but there was enough, the DA thought. With the girl's testimony. She's sixteen now, and so the judge granted the defense's motion that she be treated like an adult on the witness stand. No special treatment. And last week..." Her voice died off and she looked away.

"She killed herself?" It wasn't a difficult guess; Nick had seen it before. One of the many reasons why he preferred to work with adults even though their trauma was just as devastating and difficult to handle; at least they had a chance. Kids...kids were tough.

Deena balled up one hand into a fist then covered it with her other, bringing both up to her lips as if hiding her words. "Nick, what if, maybe, he's not coming back? What if he was trying to say goodbye in that message? What if..." A tear slid across her cheekbone, into the crease of her nose. "What if he's gone?"

Chapter 18

"I TOLD YOU NOT TO CALL." I step away from the others and keep my voice low, the cell pressed against my ear.

"It's that old man. He keeps nosing around. I almost ran into him first thing this morning, when it was barely light."

"Did he see anything?"

"No. He stayed in his truck. But I think maybe he knows something, maybe knows we're looking for it."

"We'll deal with him later, after the search is over and the cops have cleared out. Until then play your part and keep a low profile."

"What do we do with the old man? If he

comes back?"

"You're meant to be on vacation, remember? Act like fishermen. Ask him fishing questions. He's senile—give him something to do, keep him talking, and he'll forget all about where he found you or why he was there or anything he saw."

"I don't like it. And you know Hank found another of them bear traps. If we aren't careful, one of those rangers will be stumbling right into our operation. I thought that text message you had me send was meant to lead them away from here."

"It did. They shifted the search area east and north of you."

"Maybe it's time for them to find the body? That will clear them out and we can get on with business."

"I'll decide when the time is right. Just like I'll deal with the Forest Service. You keep the others calm and out of sight. Once things blow over, we'll be back in business."

"These boys are restless. You better pray it doesn't take long."

"It takes as long as it takes. We've got a good thing going—don't wreck it because you can't control your men."

"Don't you worry about me and my men. You best come through with your part or we're sunk. And if we get caught, we're taking you down with us. Just so you know."

My grip on the phone tightens into a stranglehold. It's my first time working with anyone else, but I had no choice. Doesn't mean my so-called partners will live long enough to reap the rewards of their labors—but it does mean I need to play it safe until then. "I've got it handled. Don't call again unless it's an emergency."

I hang up, visions of bloodshed calming my urge to slam the phone into pieces. I imagine how I will kill each of them, how I'll get rid of the bodies, how I'll hide all traces of my involvement and vanish into the background—until it's safe for me to leave with my bounty.

A new life, new riches, new me. Just four more bodies between me and my new beginning. Well, at least four. We'll see, maybe more.

For the first time today, my smile doesn't feel forced or fake. It feels like power. Hiding in plain sight, the serpent in the grass—I've been doing this for decades and no one's ever caught me.

No one ever will. But that's not the fun of it. The fun comes from pushing things to the very edge—kind of like how I pushed Bill over that cliff—and playing with the possibility of destruction, no matter how remote. Dancing with death.

Because if I ever am caught, imprisoned, held responsible for my actions—if everything I've done ever comes to light—then I'm doomed. It would be a fate worse than death, powerless at the hands of someone else. Never. I'll end things myself before I ever let that happen.

See? Not even death can stop me from playing my game my way. I have all the power. Just the way I like things.

Chapter 19

Forcing her breathing to slow and swallowing against a wave of bile, Lucy watched the video of the wolves again. Gleason tapped on her window, and she startled. "You can come out now."

Lucy put the laptop away and climbed down from the passenger seat. Gleason was holding a camera with a short macro lens. "Wolf tracks, six of them that I can count." He pointed to faint impressions in the dirt beside the creek bank as he knelt to photograph them. "Fresh. From the scat, they were probably here last night."

"Did they get your bear?"

"Nope, but they were ready for them." He

crept around shooting photos, and Lucy stayed behind him, out of his way.

"Them?"

"A momma and two cubs. We're trying to tag and relocate them off private land before they get into trouble with the tourists."

"But the wolves are using your traps as bait themselves."

"Yep." He sat back on his haunches, staring at the trap.

"I thought wolves hunted animals that can't fight back, like deer?"

"Usually they do. Sometimes bigger game like elk and moose—I've seen them drive an elk into deep water and then circle it, waiting it out from both sides until it's too weak to fight back. But this..." He shook his head. "It's..."

"Fascinating," Lucy finished for him. "They used our intervention and incursion into their habitat to create a new hunting strategy." She joined him at the creek bed. "Are you going to move the trap now that you know the wolves know where it is?"

"If I do, I won't know where the wolves

are or where my bears are; all I'll have is a trap sitting somewhere safe and sound. And once the wolves find it again, we'll be right back where we started."

"Maybe forget the trap? If the wolves are using it as an unfair advantage, take the bait out and close it down. Then the wolves are wasting their time waiting for a bear who's never going to come."

"Doesn't solve the problem of the bears encroaching onto human territory—"

"Or wolves coming so close. Aren't the Holmsteads llama farmers?" She remembered Judith mentioning that during the flight yesterday.

"Llamas, alpacas, and goats, a few head of cattle, horses, and this time of year, fishermen and hikers."

"It's like a tasting menu for wolves."

"The ironic thing is, humans reintroduced the wolves here back in 1995. They're only doing what comes natural—it's not like we have any right to be surprised." He stowed his camera in his pack and strode over to the trailer that the culvert trap sat on.

Lucy followed. The metal cylinder had rows of two-inch wide holes perforating the top third along both sides, the inside was smooth of any stray rivets or seams a bear could hurt itself on, and the back wall was solid steel with the lure suspended from a wire arm. She wrinkled her nose. "Smells like fish, bacon, and," she frowned, "funnel cakes?"

Gleason laughed. "My own recipe. The scientists over at Glacier have fancy lures, but I can't afford them. Bears love protein, fat, and they have a sweet tooth. So I use doughnuts soaked in bacon grease, coated in fish oil. Doesn't turn as fast as using fresh meat."

Lucy examined the trap's door mechanism. The solid metal door stood above the opening like a guillotine ready to drop. "How does it close without hurting them?"

"When the bait at the rear is triggered, the door closes. This is state-of-the-art, made for us by a guy in Missoula," Gleason said with a hint of pride. "He worked with our scientists, and even though it looks dangerous, it's rigged with safety features so the door stops if it meets any resistance like a straggling cub or even a stupid human climbing inside."

"Does that happen?"

"More often than you'd think. Usually idiots trying for a selfie to post online. But with this automated trap, we can save them from themselves." He pointed inside the front to the ceiling above the door's opening. "A webcam is activated as soon as the door closes. It also measures the temperature, so we don't have to worry about an animal overheating. And it notifies me with a text that the trap has an animal inside. All I need to do is go online, check out the camera footage, and I can monitor the animals. If it's not our target animal, I can open the door with a press of a button on my computer or phone."

"I'll bet you wait a bit on the humans," she said with a smile. He shrugged, not answering. "Wait—so each of these traps has Wi-Fi?"

He climbed over some rocks and through the huckleberry bushes to the rear of the trap.

Here was a watertight metal box attached to the trailer with wires extending up to the top of the trap, where an array of solar panels connected to a small satellite dish. "We surround each trap with trail cams, and all of them are also solar-powered and connected to the satellite Wi-Fi. Used to be we spent hundreds of man-hours checking traps, even if they were empty—or worse, having animals suffer as they waited for us to make our rounds. Now I can manage them all myself, and our data gets to the scientists immediately."

While Lucy applauded the increased efficiency and comfort for both rangers and animals, she was more interested in another aspect. "Is the Wi-Fi secured? Or could anyone use it?"

She pulled her phone out without waiting for his answer. Sure enough, it had picked up the open Wi-Fi network. "Do you have a map of all these traps and cameras?"

"Sure, give me a sec." He finished checking the trap and removed the bait, then pressed a button that resembled a doorbell at the rear of the trailer and the winch released the door. It did act like a guillotine, moving faster than Lucy had imagined, closing with a loud clang.

They returned to the truck. "If you're thinking of checking the cameras for signs of Bill, we already have volunteers doing that. No one's spotted him." He opened the glove compartment and pulled out a folded photocopied map. "This is a spare—you can keep it. I updated it last week, so it's current."

She unfolded it. He'd marked traps with circles and cameras surrounding them with X's. "Would Bill know about these?"

"Sure. The official map is in the cloud, along with real-time data about each trap." He wagged his phone. "I like to keep a few paper ones around; guess I'm old fashioned that way."

"So anyone could check and see where the cameras are?"

"Not anyone. We don't want the general public, especially your young, stupid *homo sapiens*, to know where our traps are. That's just inviting trouble. But professionals like law enforcement, researchers, registered trail guides, private landowners with traps on their property, they all have access."

He started the truck and they climbed back out of the gully, bumping along the trail. Lucy braced herself with one hand against the door and examined the map with the other. If Bill wanted to be found, he could have gone to one of the traps, used its Wi-Fi to send a message. Or if he lost his phone, he could have simply triggered one of the cameras and they'd have his location.

Which meant she was right. Bill didn't want to be found.

She circled her finger on the map, spiraling out from his last known location. Where he'd actually been seen, not just where his phone said it had been used—like Wash had demonstrated earlier, phones were too hackable, an easy way to misdirect pursuers.

A sense of calm enveloped her as she focused. This kind of hunt she understood; this kind of search she could help with.

Not a rescue operation—a manhunt.

Chapter 20

THE WATER IN THE PUDDLE ran out the morning of the second day. In addition to thirst, hunger, shock, and pain, despair began to creep into Bill's awareness. Flies swarmed his open wounds trying to feast on his blood, twice he'd chased off buzzards gawking impatiently that he wasn't dead yet, and he'd lost count of how many times he'd used his polished handcuffs as signal mirrors thinking he'd attracted one of the search planes only to watch them pass by and turn in another direction.

No water. No sign of searchers. No choice now but to drag himself out into the open, risk that the cliff wouldn't give way and tumble him farther down into the canyon. It would mean leaving the shelter that kept him relatively warm at night, but it was the only hope he had. Even though his khaki uniform blended in with the rocks, he could use his own blood to make a signal, anything to be seen and noticed.

Except...he still wasn't sure who had pushed him off the cliff. At first all he'd remembered was taking pictures with his phone, getting too close to the edge, stepping back—and then a jolt like lightning. But then he could swear he'd felt someone push him. And lightning should have left more marks on his body, like exit wounds.

Someone had tried to kill him. Would they come back? No, after two days, they had to assume he was dead. Which meant no more dawdling; it was time to move.

He wrapped his belt around both legs to splint them. The pain knocked him out for, given the position of the sun, a good hour. Now came the hard part—rotating his body free of the crevice so that he could belly crawl and drag his useless legs behind him. All with one good hand. Except he was starting to worry about that left hand—his shoulder had begun to ache, and he couldn't figure out why. But that was the least of his worries.

First he lay as flat as possible and did a weird butt scoot, bumping his legs over the rocks, just far enough to free his torso from the space between the boulder and the cliff wall. Then he pushed himself back up against the outside of the boulder, his entire body now in the sun for the first time in two days. His head pounded and he was so dizzy it was a good thing he had nothing to throw up, although that didn't stop him from dry-heaving, which only added to his agony as his ribs protested.

Basking in the sunshine, that deserved a brief rest, he told himself, as he choked back the nausea. Just close his eyes for a moment or three.

The sound of a plane's engine woke him, the sun now past its zenith. Hell, he'd lost two more hours. At this rate he'd make it around the boulder by next week. But he was more exposed now, with nothing between him and the plane. He fumbled his handcuffs from his chest pocket, polished them on his shirttail, folded them to maximize their surface area, and looked into the sun, trying to catch the light. The sun was so bright he had to slit his one good eye and still saw red, but there was a definite glint reflected from the metal handcuffs—was it enough? Did the pilot see?

At first he thought the plane was headed right for him. He kept signaling, frantically searching for the best angle, waving his hand overhead to catch the light. They're coming! They saw it!

The plane kept coming, closer and closer. Bill let hope drown out his pain and stretched as far as he could, still signaling, waiting for a response. *C'mon, give me a little wing-wag, let me know you see me. C'mon, c'mon, just a little closer...*

And then the plane, just like all the others he'd spotted, veered away to the east. Always to the north and the east—as if they were intentionally searching in the exact opposite direction.

He slumped back, the glimmer of hope

doused. Exhaustion overwhelmed him. This was as far as he could make it. He leaned back against the boulder and closed his eyes, the sun casting his vision in red. It wouldn't take long to get a sunburn, so he added that to his list of things Deena would chide him for when he saw her again.

Why were they searching in the wrong direction? The best he could come up with was that they were basing the search radius off his last phone call—when he'd left a message for Lucy after he'd left the Holmsteads' ranch. Damn, he'd sidetracked up to this meadow on his way back to the station, so he'd never had the chance to run a background check on the pair of so-called fishermen camping out by the river on Gus's land. He hadn't liked the look of those two—they'd said they were engineers from the oil fields in North Dakota, here on vacation. Which could well be true, but they sure as hell weren't fishermen.

Had they followed him? All the way from Gus's? If they'd wanted to, there were plenty of chances to jump him there—but they'd be the top of the suspect list. But why? He hadn't seen anything suspicious; if he had, he would have arrested them then and there.

Besides, they'd only been around for a few days. Which meant they couldn't have anything to do with his killer—if there actually was a serial killer. So far all the cases he'd dug up could be explained by natural causes or accidents; but wouldn't that be perfect for a serial killer? Hiding in plain sight, targeting rural areas lacking the forensic resources of the big city?

And Dr. Carruthers, the coroner over in Idaho County—Judith Keenan had caught him making several mistakes. Mistakes that seemed obvious once she uncovered them. Who knew how many more there were? County coroner—the perfect job for a serial killer. How easy to get away with murder when you're the one in charge of the death investigations and death certificates.

But if it was Carruthers, how had he gotten all the way from Grangeville and just happened to track Bill down when he'd gone to scout a new huckleberry site for Deena? No way could he have known Bill was coming here—Bill hadn't even decided it until the last minute when he drove past the Forest Service road leading up to the meadow. Unless Carruthers somehow tracked his phone? There were all sorts of apps that could do that—some of them you didn't even need to be near the phone, you just needed the access code. Lord knew, he'd stood near Carruthers enough times at death scenes and in his office. It would have been easy for the coroner to steal his code.

As the afternoon wore on, Bill stopped sweating despite the heat. His mouth was parched and he'd lost all his spit. Worse, the buzzards had returned—three of them now, cackling like Macbeth's witches as they paced the boulder over his head.

Bill didn't have his phone. He'd lost it when he fell—he remembered it flying from his hand as he spun over the cliff's edge, his body twisting with the electrical shock. He had the vaguest impression it had flown toward solid ground rather than falling through the air with him. Maybe it was sitting up there, his pretty pictures still filling the screen, just waiting for someone to find it. There was no cell signal out here, but shouldn't the GPS still have worked? He couldn't remember if this was one of the dead zones for satellite reception or not.

Anyway, he had no phone to use to record a last message. He didn't really want Deena to see him this way, and his voice was gone. So he pried his one good eye open and used his one good hand to fish his notepad with its tiny pencil from his pants pocket, and with a trembling wrong-handed scrawl, began to write a farewell letter to his wife.

It was short—not because he didn't have a whole universe to say to her, but because any words that came to mind seemed so tiny and meaningless compared to the way he felt about her.

In the end, all he managed was:

Deena,

The bright star who guided me, kept me warm, saved my soul, and stole my heart. You are my life, my love, my everything.

I'm sorry, I tried, just ran out of time and luck.

Love forever, Bill

CHAPTER 21

AS GLEASON DROVE THEM ACROSS the Holmsteads' sprawling land—past a small air strip, several cabins along the banks of the river, fenced in pastures with llamas grazing on one side of the road and horses on the other—Lucy couldn't stop wondering: why didn't Bill want to be found? She spread the large-scale map of the search out over her lap and noted all the grids checked off, all centered around the location Bill's phone was reported to be at when he'd sent that text to Judith yesterday.

What if it had all been a waste of time? A misdirection? She focused on where he'd been last seen—the same place his last voicemail to her had originated from two days ago. Three miles west of the text's location. Three miles didn't seem like that much, but it translated to a huge swath of land now suddenly on the outer margin of the search area.

"Gus Holmstead was the last person to see Bill, right?"

"The last person to talk with Bill," Gleason corrected her.

"Wait. Then who saw him last?"

"Judith Keenan. She was here checking on an animal and happened to follow Bill out. He turned east when they hit the road, and he stopped his car—from the GPS coordinates, he must have stopped to call and leave that last voicemail on your phone. She headed in the other direction, back to town. No one has seen him since."

"She didn't talk to Bill? Ask him where he was going?"

"No. It was a sheer coincidence she was able to verify the visual sighting—before she came forward, we'd been working from the GPS map the phone company gave us."

"Can I see that?"

"Sure, it's on the laptop." He slowed the truck and they bumped off road. Lucy glanced up to see that they were driving down a dry creek bed. The river must have diverted away from it a long time ago because the sandy loam was packed hard. "There's another trap near the river I want to check."

She opened his laptop and clicked on the file for the phone's GPS map. It showed Bill's movements—or rather his phone's—for the past week: a high-density zigzag trail from his home to the center of town—the sheriff's station—then a kaleidoscope of random curves crisscrossing out from that radius. Calls and patrol routes. The path to the Holmstead ranch was denser, indicating he'd gone out there several times.

There was an arrow marking where he'd called her from to leave that final voicemail, almost exactly where she'd parked his truck this morning, a spot where she'd fortuitously noted both cell and Wi-Fi coverage, weak as they were. Probably all the spots like that were well known to the locals.

No readings for over an hour—maybe he'd

stayed in the same spot, having lunch? Or turned the phone off so it would charge faster? Or he'd entered a dead zone with no cell or satellite signal. When the signal returned, it was back at the same spot and then moved east along the Magruder Corridor. After almost two miles, it stopped. No more GPS data—the phone had been turned off when the state police asked the cell company to try to locate it. But then the next day there was one data point, another mile farther east and north, in the wilderness area. The timing fit with the text he'd sent. Then nothing.

What the hell was he doing up there? Or rather his phone? Maybe he hadn't sent that text at all. She didn't like the way the phone was turned off then on again just to send the one text that re-routed the search. If Bill were trying to hide, why chance turning the phone back on? He didn't need to send the text as a decoy to misdirect the search teams, not with all this wilderness to hide in and a full day's head start.

Unless it hadn't been Bill, but someone

else manipulating them. Who? Why?

"What the hell do those fools think they're doing?" Gleason asked, hitting the brakes so hard the truck fishtailed as it shimmied to a stop. He was out of the truck before Lucy could stow the laptop and open her door to join him.

In front of them, near the river, were two large canvas tents on platforms and a fire ring with three men gathered around it. But that wasn't what had Gleason so furious. It was the pile of trash, including empty food containers stacked up beside a pair of large ice chests.

"You do realize you're rolling out the red carpet, inviting bears by leaving all that trash out?" he told them, his voice strained, posture angry. "Not to mention how unsafe it is to be doing any kind of food prep or storage so close to camp? I know the Holmsteads gave you all the rules—since this is their property, they're on the hook for any damage."

Lucy caught up to the ranger, taking a stand behind him and to his left. She watched the three men, paying particular attention to their hands and stance—one of them was one of the geologic engineers who'd flown in with her and Nick. She didn't see any weapons on the men, other than clasp knifes hooked onto their belts, but there were two AR-15 rifles propped against the log they'd been using as a seat, one of them with thermal imaging sights. A lot of firepower for engineers on a fishing trip.

"This is prime area for grizzly, black bear, wolves, and mountain lion," Gleason continued. "I know that sounds romantic to city folk, but trust me, you do not want to be inviting them into your camp."

Where was the fourth man, Davenport? Lucy wondered, stepping back to try to get a look inside both tents. They were empty except for pickaxes, shovels, and a variety of equipment boxes. She remembered the ground-penetrating radar unit they'd brought onto the plane. Davenport had said they were on a working vacation. What exactly were they looking for?

"Sorry, officer." One of the men finally took the lead. He nodded to the pistol holstered at Gleason's hip. "We didn't mean any harm."

"It's Ranger, Ranger Gleason. Forest Service."

"But isn't this private land? I mean, we paid to be here—"

"The Holmsteads give us access. In fact, we have a bear trap about a mile and a half downstream from here. If I'd known you all were baiting them yourselves—" Gleason cut his words short, pressing his lips together. "Look, we just don't want anyone to get hurt." He glanced at the two semi-automatic rifles. "And you know you can't take those off the Holmstead property. There's no hunting right now; season's closed."

Movement from upstream caught Lucy's eye. The fourth man, Davenport. He was pushing a piece of equipment the size of a lawnmower. The GPR unit. When he saw Lucy and Gleason, he left the unit and jogged to join his partners. "Well, hi there, Lucy, former FBI agent. Good to see you again. What brings you guys all the way out here?"

"The man's upset we've been cooking and

leaving the trash out," the other man from the plane told him.

"I told you guys to collect the trash and burn it." Davenport turned to Gleason. "I'm so sorry. We're not used to these primitive conditions, roughing it. It's fun the first few days, but then—" He shrugged, holding his hands up. "Is burning it good enough? We've been storing the food in special bear cans we bought in town. Is there something else we should be doing?"

"Yeah, a lot." Gleason gestured to the trash pile, and Davenport joined him. Lucy skipped the lecture on basic camp skills and took the opportunity to study the rest of the site. The other men divided, two joining Davenport and Gleason and one watching her as he sat on the log within arm's reach of the rifles.

She didn't care what they called themselves or how much fancy equipment they had, these guys were not geologists. At least not the law-abiding kind. But neither she nor Gleason had jurisdiction here—and she couldn't see any laws that they were breaking. Still, her senses were on high alert, scanning for danger, uncomfortable with the fact that she and Gleason were outnumbered and outgunned.

Gleason and Davenport seemed to come to an understanding. "I'll stop back by a bit later, make sure you don't need any more help."

The men frowned at that even as Davenport nodded and extended a hand for Gleason to shake. "Thanks so much, we really appreciate it. Don't worry, it won't happen again. We'll get this all cleaned up and taken care of right away."

Gleason nodded and turned back to the truck. Lucy kept watch on the men until he was safely inside. "You coming?" he shouted to her.

"Yeah, sorry," she said, backing up to her side of the truck, never losing sight of the men. She climbed in, and he spun the wheel. "What about the bear trap?"

"There's nothing on the cameras, and I can swap the bait out later. That gives me a reason to check up on those guys. I'll never understand why people pay good money to go on vacation without knowing a damn thing about the place they're visiting."

"I thought the Holmsteads hired them. They're geological engineers. Nick and I flew in with two of them."

"Hired them for what?" He considered that for a moment. "A few years ago, they found some fossils down in the canyon south of here—with the drought, more of the bedrock is exposed, so maybe Amy or Gus came across something."

"Like the dinosaurs they've found in Montana?"

"They need the money. Maybe these guys can help them dig it up or find more."

They pulled up to a farmhouse between two large barns and an equipment shed. A young woman was working on a tractor while an elderly man looked over her shoulder.

"Gus, Amy," Gleason hailed them as he hopped out of the truck. Lucy joined him. "This is Lucy—she's helping in the search for Bill, and would love to talk to you."

Amy looked up, a crescent wrench clutched in one hand. "You're Nick's wife. He was on the team yesterday." She stepped away from the tractor, leading them out of earshot of the older man who took over the work on the engine. As they walked, she aimed a smile intended solely for Gleason. One that he returned readily, Lucy couldn't help but notice. Guess that explained why an overworked Forest Service employee with a huge territory to administer somehow managed to spend so much time on private land. "You'll be wanting to talk with Gus, then."

"You weren't here when Bill came by?"

"Nope. I never saw Bill, not after getting him and Gus coffee that morning. I went out with Judith to check on Jericho. Bill was gone when I got back."

"Jericho?" Lucy asked.

"One of our pack llamas. He came up lame a few weeks ago; had a rock stuck in his foot. It's been slow to heal, and Judith was worried it might lead to infection, so she's been keeping a real close eye on him. Even put a GPS collar on him in case he comes up lame again."

"Speaking of lame," Gleason said, "those

guys camped down at the river are doing a shit job policing their trash and food. I read them the riot act, but I figured you might want to check in on them."

"Yeah, sorry. With the search and everything, I haven't gone down there. They said not to bother them, so I didn't even think—but I'll keep an eye on them, and I can take the gator down and haul a load of trash out if need be."

"They said they're geological engineers," Lucy said. "Do you know what they're looking for?"

Amy frowned. "Gus made all their arrangements, and said not to ask any questions, that they wanted their privacy. All I know is Gus said it would be worth our while." She glanced over her shoulder to the tractor. Gus had his head and shoulders down into the machinery's innards. "He's up to something; I'm not sure what. But I can try to find out."

"Whoever they are, they don't know squat about camping," Gleason said. "I shut down the trap on the north branch—the wolves were targeting it. But with those guys so close, I think I'll come back later and shut down the one in the west canyon. Just to be on the safe side."

"Thanks, Gleason." Amy turned to Lucy, lowering her voice. "Just to warn you, Gus can be kind of...single-minded? I've asked him about what he and Bill talked about, so have Judith and Gleason, even Judge Carson came by. He's not senile, just kinda set in his ways, focused on what he thinks is important and tends to ignore everything else."

"Stubborn and compulsive," Gleason said.

"Yeah, okay," Amy admitted. "But a lot of that is because he has a such hard time getting around because of his hip. It kills him to feel helpless, that he can't go roaming the countryside like he once did."

Lucy nodded her understanding. "Bill obviously thought he had something to contribute."

Amy beamed. "He used to visit a few times a week just to talk to Gus about the goings on around here after he left home. Guess since Bill didn't have any family of his own left here, coming back he felt a bit lost. And of course, the Beacheys and the Magruders have always had a special bond."

"Gus is descended from Lloyd Magruder," Gleason told Lucy. She still didn't understand why people here made such a point of remembering a murder victim but not the man who brought his killers to justice in a time when justice was rare and hard to come by.

Amy led the way back to the tractor. "Gus, come on out now. I have someone I want you to meet."

Gus's voice echoed against the tractor's hood as he strained against a stubborn nut. "No time for tea parties, girl. We've got to get this thing running."

"She's a friend of Bill's. She needs your help."

There was a clang of metal against metal and a muffled curse. Gus straightened up, pulled his hands from the engine—minus the wrench he'd dropped—and turned to Lucy. He was wiry, his skin marked by time spent in the sun, and although his thinning white hair proclaimed him to be in his eighties, the gleam in his eye was that of a much younger man.

"Friend—are you Lucy?" He reached a grease-stained hand out for her to shake. His grip was strong despite a tremor that shook his forearm.

"Yes, I am. I'm trying to retrace Bill's steps, as well as the cases he was interested in. I found some notes in his home office that seemed to suggest he was talking to you about some old investigations?"

Gus sucked on his teeth, then turned to limp toward the house. When Lucy didn't follow immediately, he glanced back over his shoulder. "Well, c'mon then. Amy, you and that boy of yours can finish fixing the tractor. This is Bill's FBI friend, and we got business to discuss."

Chapter 22

The Holmstead house was a traditional two-story that would have been at home on any Pennsylvania farm. Gus led her up the porch, through the front door, and past the formal sitting room to the less formal eat-in kitchen at the rear of the house. The kitchen faced south, its bay window overlooking the sprawling pasture where the llama roamed. Some were big and stout, obviously pack animals. Others had more elegant features and long hair in a variety of deep, rich shades. The alpacas raised for wool—or was it hair when it didn't come from a sheep? Lucy had no clue.

"Are alpacas llamas or are llamas alpacas?" she asked, as Gus poured two mugs of coffee for them and joined her at the table by the window. His limp was severe enough that he sloshed coffee almost over the brim of the cups but his glare sat her down when she rose to help.

“Don’t make fun of my buddies,” he chided her. “They saved this place. Back when my wife was still alive, twenty some years ago, we were about to go under. The economy was in the toilet, and no one wanted to buy a place like this out in the middle of nowhere—not with all the government regulations on the land surrounding us. No one cared that a hundred and fifty years ago there was supposed to be enough gold on this land to start a country of your own.”

“Gold?” Deena had mentioned something about Bill searching for hidden treasure. Before he became obsessed with the idea of a serial killer prowling his county.

“You know about Lloyd Magruder, how he was murdered for a few sacks of gold dust? Well, that was nothing compared to the gold his brother found. Right here on this land.”

"Where?"

He chuckled. "That's the problem. Damn fool buried it to hide it from claim jumpers, but then got lost in a blizzard and died on his way home before he could tell anyone where he'd hid it. It was a miracle his poor wife was even able to hang onto the land at all. But she did. Just like my Betty, she wouldn't give up. Betty, she got the whole llama thing up and running. She dug in, joined groups on the internet—there weren't so many back then—asked questions of anyone who had something to offer. We were doing just fine until she died, and I—" He waved a futile hand at his legs. He took a long sip of his coffee.

Lucy waited. She could offer empty words of comfort, but to a man like Gus, she sensed they'd be meaningless.

"You're like Bill," he finally said. "A good listener. Not like those other fools who keep coming by. I tell them they're looking in the wrong place, but no one believes me."

"Why do you think they're looking in the wrong place?"

"Bill. That morning he was here, we talked about all sorts of things. Like always. Where the huckleberries were ripe for picking." He stopped. "Amy will have my hide. Hang on." Before Lucy could offer to help, he'd pushed back from the table, gotten up, and brought back a plate of cornbread and a jar of jam. "Sorry about that. I've no appetite these days, and sometimes forget my manners. Go on, now. Amy will count 'em when she comes in, and she'll be insulted if you don't take some."

Lucy smiled. The cornbread had a delicate golden crust and was light and fluffy, the scent of cinnamon wafting from it. She slathered a piece with the jam and tried it. "Delicious," she said before she finished chewing. And she meant it.

"I told Amy where to find the best huckleberries. It's her first try at making jam, but she did good."

"She did," Lucy agreed, helping herself to a second piece. "So you were saying..."

"Right. Bill and I, we were talking about cases—I used to be a county commissioner.

Thankless job. Everyone wants something, but there's never enough to go around. The fire department and ambulance crew are volunteer. Half our deputies are volunteer reserve. Harriet, the sheriff's department dispatcher, actually draws her pay from the federal because she's also our postmistress. Constant robbing Peter to pay Paul."

"They were lucky to have you."

He snorted. "Same three people run for election every year—power hungry. Nelson Vrynchek, who owns an equipment company, wants first dibs on any new logging or road maintenance contracts. Mickey Durham, he always runs for treasurer—he's cooking the books, I'm sure, but no one's been able to catch him. And Verna Highsmith, she's been secretary for going on two decades, I swear just to be first to get the best gossip. The other three seats are at-large members and if no one runs for them, we hold a lottery of registered voters who are permanent residents. That's how bad it's gotten around here—all's that left is a bunch of old folks like me, and no one gives a damn."

"Was Bill interested in becoming a commissioner?"

"No, no. He was interested in when I was one. You know he's been digging into all the death investigations—determined to find a real case he can sink his teeth into. Poor guy, only been here a year and already bored to tears. I'm not sure he'll last. Anyway, that's why they're looking in the wrong place for Bill. Amy told me where they were searching; said it was based on tracking his phone. It's everything east and north of here. Which is wrong. I don't know nothing about phone tracking, but I know tracking people. And you start with where they were last seen and where they were going."

"And Bill wasn't going east or north?"

"No, that's what I'm trying to tell you. A couple of times when I was commissioner, we had to call in the coroner over in Idaho County to handle a death because Judith was out of town. Carruthers. What a horse's ass. Took forever to get here, insisted on all these fancy tests—that came out of our budget—and twice he got it wrong. And he's an M.D. When Judith got back and reviewed everything, she figured things out and set him straight. We're lucky to have her. She's the smartest doctor—human or animal or any other kind—I've ever met."

"So Bill was interested in Judith's cases?" Lucy asked, trying to steer him back on track without curtailing his thoughts. Often it was something a witness considered irrelevant that ended up breaking a case.

"Not just Judith's—that doctor over in Grangeville as well. That's where Bill said he was headed. Said he wanted to talk to the Idaho County coroner." He leaned forward, dropping his voice as if someone might be listening. "You see, Bill thought he was after a serial killer. Someone hiding in plain sight, he said. Said he figured a killer wouldn't care about lines on a map, they'd be killing in both counties, maybe even up on the rez. Anywhere they could get away with murder."

Chapter 23

Before Lucy could ask Gus more about Bill's suspicions, her phone rang. She answered it—no cell bars, but it was connecting through the Wi-Fi just fine.

"It's me," Nick said, his voice hushed and urgent as if he didn't want anyone to overhear him. "How fast can you get to Deena's?"

Once she got a ride back to where Bill's truck was parked... "About twenty-thirty minutes." She was guessing, but it wasn't far in mileage; only the roads were so abysmal and none of them ran in a straight line. "Why?"

"The district ranger who's leading the search called. Said he was coming to talk with Deena."

She was silent for a long moment. Good news you didn't have to deliver in person; in fact, you wanted to get good news to loved ones as fast as possible. "I'm on my way." She hung up and turned to Gus. "Thank you—for the cornbread and for the information. I promise you, I'll check it out as soon as I can."

The old man reached a hand out and Lucy shook it, feeling as if she were sealing a formal deal. "You find Bill. He's needed here."

"I'll do my best," she promised. Lucy made a point of never promising anything she couldn't deliver, but this seemed a safe bet. "Call me if you think of anything."

"Put your number in my phone, then I don't have to bother Amy for it." He slid a wide-screen smartphone across the table to her. She entered her info and handed it back to him. The font was set so large her phone number took up the entire screen. Maybe Gus had more problems than just a bum hip. The joys of getting old. She stood, her weight landing heavily on her bad ankle. "Take care, Gus."

Amy and Gleason were still huddled over

the tractor, side by side, their heads almost touching. "Gleason, do you mind driving me back to Bill's truck? Nick just called—your boss is headed over to Deena's house. He said he had to talk to her in person."

Both Amy and Gleason frowned at the news. "Nothing on the radio that they found him," Gleason said, touching the radio at his belt. "Maybe he just wants to introduce himself since he's taking over from me."

"Let's hope." Lucy climbed into the ranger's truck, then waited as he said goodbye to Amy. A few minutes later they were rattling down the gravel road leading north to the Magruder Corridor. As they drove, she noted the landmarks—the gnarled dead tree marking the trail to the first bear trap, the better-traveled track that led south to the river where the geologists were camped. She never did have a chance to ask Gus what they were surveying. Not that it was any of her business. "Do you think he might be calling off the search? It's been three days."

"But only one day since the text

yesterday," Gleason reminded her.

"Gus says you all have been looking in the wrong direction."

"I know; he told me. He said Bill would be heading west to Grangeville because he wanted to talk to Dr. Carruthers. Only problem is, Judith was at the ranch while Bill was there and left right after him, and she saw his Jeep parked facing east—just about exactly where you parked this morning. One of the few places where it's easy to get a call out this far outside of town."

"That fits with his last call to me, according to the GPS tracking. Then his phone went dead, and there was no more tracking data."

"Which wouldn't make sense if he turned around to head west to Grangeville because after the first few miles, he'd be heading into an area of good cell service with no GPS blind spots. Unlike heading east along the Corridor. You lose both out there."

"I thought GPS coverage was good—isn't that why hikers use it?"

"Not everywhere. Like down in the deep canyons, the rocks block it, just like brick and cement walls can in a city. But it's good enough when you climb out that most folks only notice a lag in their maps refreshing—most mapping apps store enough info that it's not a big deal." He tapped the steering wheel as he thought. "But still, I checked with Dr. Carruthers' office. Turns out he's on vacation until the end of next week. Bill would never drive that far without calling ahead first, so he would have known that. Or, more likely, he already knew it—he and the Idaho County Sheriff keep each other up to date with things like that."

"So Judith is covering for Dr. Carruthers?"

Gleason rolled his eyes. "Not any more. The last time she was out of town, a couple in an RV died up at the Willowbank Campground just outside of town. Carruthers found traces of a suspicious powder and called it a homicide—cyanide poisoning. He said it was almost impossible to test for with an autopsy, but he was certain. Then when Judith got back and checked it out for herself, she found the exhaust was leaking into the cabin, tested for carbon monoxide, and it turned out she was right. He was super embarrassed since he'd called in the State Police and their crime scene unit, had folks running this way and that searching for a killer who wasn't there. Ever since then, he gets a doctor from Lewiston to cover for him, and she tries not to go out of town."

They reached the intersection, Bill's truck exactly where she'd left it a few hours ago. Lucy hopped out. "Can I keep the bear map?" she asked. "My daughter will think it's cool. It might be the only souvenir she gets from this trip."

"Sure. The website password is on the bottom—she can log in, check out the live stream, even sign up to get alerts when a trap is active."

"Can she see the wolves, too? Knowing Megan, they'll be much more fascinating to her than the bears."

He chuckled. "Typical bloodthirsty teenager, they always root for the predators.

Sure, all the videos are archived. And if she's really interested, we're always looking for volunteers to help review the footage. Not just for predators but to look for patterns of all the animals using those trails."

"Thanks. Take care." She left and got into Bill's truck, then did a three-point turn to head back west toward Deena's.

As she drove, she pictured a map of Bill's route according to his cell records. The text yesterday—if that hadn't come from him, why send it? What purpose had it served?

It moved the search area farther north and east. Why would someone want that? To send the searchers away from Bill? That would suggest he was still alive and in a location south or west of the search area.

The geologists were also south of the search area and to the west. But if Gus had hired them to survey his own land, why go to such a convoluted method to steer the searchers clear of the survey? And how would they have gotten access to Bill's phone?

Still, she wished she'd gotten the full

names of all the geologists so she could have Wash run a background check. Judith would know the two who'd flown in with Lucy and Nick; Lucy would ask her next time she saw her. But those two had solid alibis—they'd been in North Dakota the day Bill vanished and in the plane with her, Nick, and Judith when the last text came through.

Which brought her to the only other reason she could think for someone to send that last text and make it look like it was from Bill: to establish an alibi. But what good would an alibi do anyone without a body to determine time of death?

Then she thought of one final reason—the one she'd been avoiding all along. The text was actually from Bill. He really was acting irrationally, staying out a full night before sending it, maybe contemplating what he was about to do. And the text was his final goodbye.

She shook her head, almost missing the turn to Deena and Bill's cabin. No. She didn't believe it. Not because she believed Bill wasn't vulnerable to depression, but his messages to her—he'd sounded excited, involved. Not like someone pushed to the brink of despair.

Plus, he would never do that to Deena. To leave her to worry for days not knowing... He knew what that kind of waiting did to a cop's wife, how painful it was even if there was good news at the end. No, if he were going to kill himself, he'd protect Deena from finding the body and from any uncertainty.

At least she hoped so.

She arrived at the cabin a little more than forty minutes after Nick's call. She'd just parked and gotten out of the truck when a middle-aged man in a Forest Service uniform, complete with Smokey Bear hat, came out of the front door, shutting it carefully behind him. His expression was grim as he nodded at Lucy without saying a word and got into a forest green Tahoe.

She watched him drive away, bracing herself for what might be waiting inside, and then climbed the steps to the porch and knocked on the door. Nick opened it and joined her outside. "I'm glad you came."

"Did they find something?"

"No. That's the problem. No sign of Bill or his Jeep. The ranger wants to refocus away from the forest and the ground search, and concentrate on roads instead."

"Is that his call to make?"

"That's why he came. To discuss it with Deena—explain that it wasn't giving up, just working the percentages that Bill was last seen with his vehicle, and since they haven't found it, odds are that Bill is still with it. Which means roads, not forest."

She frowned. It made sense—in fact, it had been her instinct this morning, to treat the search more like a manhunt, as if Bill were a fugitive on the run, not wanting to be found. But it still didn't feel right.

"Anyway," Nick continued. "Officially, as acting sheriff, Judith has the final say. They already alerted a tri-state area and the border to be on a lookout for Bill's Jeep, so she wants to continue the ground search. Especially with the text Bill sent yesterday. They got into it right in front of Deena—"

"Is she okay?"

"Not really." He hesitated. "Her mom and sister have been preparing her for the worst. Including that maybe that text from Bill was a suicide note. I guess he's been pretty upset lately about a case in Denver where a child victim ended up killing herself when it fell apart."

"So you think he could—it's a possibility?"

"Who's to say? That's the problem. There won't be any answers for anyone until he's found. Anyway, Judith convinced Deena to take a sleeping pill—she'd been up for almost three days straight."

Lucy glanced at the house, ashamed at the relief that washed over her. She was no good at sitting vigil. In fact, she couldn't help but think that maybe Nick had been right last night, and she'd made things worse for Deena instead of helping.

"I saw Bill's office," Nick said, effortlessly following her thoughts. "I'm not sure you were totally off track."

"That there might be a serial killer?"

"That Bill *thought* he might have found a serial killer. That doesn't make it true. You know how easy it can be to make connections that aren't real."

"This is Bill. He's not delusional."

"I'm not saying he was, I'm just saying we don't know what was going on in his mind. Particularly in the last few days before he vanished."

She blew her breath out in frustration. "Did you eat lunch yet?"

"There's plenty of food inside."

But also Deena's family. And Judith, who seemed to revel in hovering, feeding off crisis. Although that wasn't fair, Lucy had never had a chance to see the veterinarian in any other situation. Still... "Let's go back to town and check out the café. Maybe we can talk to the folks at the sheriff's station and see what they thought about Bill's serial killer theory."

CHAPTER 24

THERE WAS ONLY ONE OTHER CUSTOMER at the cafe, a white-haired man enjoying a BLT as he read a newspaper—a real paper newspaper. No screens in sight. The sight made Nick feel as if he'd stepped into an Edward Hopper painting.

"Your parents convinced Megan to go camping," Lucy told him as they waited for their meals.

"*Camping* camping? Or a hike that ends up at a day spa?"

"Actual tent and sleeping bag camping. She said she wanted to see the places you went when you were growing up. Your photos inspired her."

"Maybe she'll have fun—like she did

when she was little. Remember that trip when she was what, three?"

"It stormed so hard half the mountain slid down past our tent."

"But you showed her how to make little clay pots with the mud and cooked them in the fire. Then we zipped the sleeping bags together and we all cuddled inside the tent." Megan still had that tiny lop-sided reddish clay pot sitting on her bookcase alongside her Kempo and shooting trophies.

Lucy smiled. "I remember. And that night after the storm passed, we sat up counting shooting stars and making wishes."

"It felt like we were the only people in the universe." He reached for her hand. "We've been blessed with so many of those perfect moments. More than most."

She ducked her head, unable to meet his eyes. But she couldn't hide her thoughts, not from him. Because for every perfect moment, there'd been just as many harrowing moments with her family worrying about her. The price of her doing her job—a price he and Megan paid.

"You heard Bill's messages." She changed the subject, although not really. "Do you really think that was a man getting ready to kill himself?"

Their food arrived—a salad with grilled chicken for him, a buffalo burger for her—saving him from answering right away. "I'm not sure. That case from back in Denver, the victim who committed suicide, sounded like it really threw him. And this obsession with uncovering a possible serial killer—"

"Obsession?" Lucy jerked her chin up. "You think he truly was obsessed? Maybe even delusional?"

Nick chose his words carefully. "You know I can't diagnose anyone with the scraps of information we have, but he definitely sounded driven."

"Gus said he and Bill met several times to discuss what Gus remembered of those old cases. He was skeptical at first, but by the end, he believed Bill. That there was something more going on."

A lonely, bored old man anxious to be

involved in some drama, was Nick's first thought. But that was the problem—first impressions were all he had to go on. Except... "Let's start with the Bill we know. He talked to you about his cases back in Denver. Did he ever seem obsessive with them? Likely to let his imagination carry him to extremes?"

"Like convinced there's a serial killer hiding in plain sight in rural Idaho?" She took a bite of her burger—it was so thick, she had to mash it down to fit into her mouth. She chewed slowly and thought. "No. If anything, I'm more the type to run off chasing a theory, getting obsessed, than Bill ever was. He's cautious, painstaking, and meticulous the way he builds his cases, double-checking every piece of data."

"Let's assume he hasn't changed since we saw him last. Does what you saw in his home office jive with the investigator you just described?"

She closed her eyes for a moment, no doubt imagining the chaos of Bill's office. "Yes," she finally said, her expression clearing for the first time since they'd arrived. "I know it looked jumbled and unorganized, but he saw a pattern there. But I think he wasn't certain, which is why he was running down every bit of information. Talking to people like Gus who were around during the killings. Reviewing the coroners' reports and lab results." She met his gaze head on. "Nick, he wasn't obsessed or delusional. He was slowly, painstakingly working a case."

"Okay, so where do we go from here?"

"His laptop was missing from his home office—Deena thought he either had it with him in the Jeep or had left it at the sheriff's station." She took another bite, staring out the window across the empty street to the old bank building that housed the Magruder County government offices. "Maybe he also had written case notes—Bill was old school like that."

"You want to search his office at the sheriff's station?"

Her grin was the first true smile he'd seen since they'd left Pittsburgh. "Do you feel like providing a diversion?"

How could he say no?

Once they'd finished eating, they wandered over to the sheriff's office. Which was also the county clerk's office, the post office, and the county-wide dispatcher's office for first responders. The lobby still resembled the bank the offices had displaced, with a waiting area separated from the work area behind the former tellers' counter.

Only one person was there—Harriet, the older woman who had helped to coordinate the search yesterday. A bell chimed as the door closed behind them, and Harriet turned from a wall-sized map where she was pasting colored sticky notes. Radio chatter from the search served as background noise. Her smile of welcome froze and died when she saw Lucy. The two women had definitely not gotten along yesterday when Lucy tried to convince Harriet to add her to a search party—and Harriet now bristled.

"FBI or not, I'm not sending you out with a team," she said, before Lucy could even offer a greeting.

"Actually, Deena sent us," Nick said,

leaning across the counter with its postal meter, pay station, and computer. "She asked if we could gather up a few of Bill's personal items from his office."

"Just a few photos and the like," Lucy added, staying behind Nick.

"Not that she's expecting the worst," Nick hastened to add. "But if she has to go on TV and make a public appeal—"

Harriet nodded at that, her eyes wide with the thought of TV crews here in quiet Poet Springs. "Sure, I get that."

The phone rang and Harriet turned to get it. "911, what's your emergency?" She listened. "No. Walter, I don't care how inconvenient it is, I'm not sending the fire department all the way out to your place to climb up your roof and adjust your satellite for you. I don't care if you are missing Judge Judy, we've got real emergencies going on around here."

Lucy made a swooshing "Relax, I got it" gesture and pushed through the swinging gate at the end of the counter. She passed the desks to Bill's office in the corner behind Harriet.

"No, we haven't found him yet." Harriet followed Lucy's progress with a frown but then pulled her focus back to the phone. "I know, it's been too long. I'll add your prayers to the list. Now don't you go climbing up there by yourself, you'll fall and break a hip for sure. Once the search teams are done for the day, I'll send Campbell out. You're welcome." She hung up.

"Wow, you really do do it all around here," Nick said. He nodded at the gate, and Harriet smiled her permission. He joined her at the map, conveniently keeping her back to Bill's office. "What do all these notes mean?"

"These are sectors where we've done hasty searches." She pointed to the pink slips of paper. "These we've finished more in-depth grid searches." There were considerably fewer of the yellow notes. "And these," she indicated a variety of thumbtacks, "are reported sightings—none of which have checked out. Folks just want to get involved, feel useful, I guess."

The phone rang again. "911—" She paused. "No, this is the right number. Doc

Judith is busy helping with the search, so she's forwarded all her calls here. Is it an emergency?" She leaned over her desk, scribbling on a notepad. "You have the semen and want to schedule—oh, not until next week? Okay, I'll pass the message on, but give her time to get back to you, right now she's got a lot on her plate." She shook her head. "Some folks think more of their animals than they do their own neighbors."

"Judith is pretty amazing," Nick said. "Running her practice, which obviously takes her all over—"

"You should see her come calving season, zipping all over in that little plane of hers."

"Plus being county coroner and now acting sheriff."

"Don't forget running that motel her husband saddled her with." She shook her head in regret. "That damn thing's a money pit. The poor woman will never be free of it. Don't know what he was thinking."

From the light in her eyes, he'd found a topic that would hold her interest. "She told us about her husband's death."

"Such a shame. They'd only been here a few years, but he seemed like a nice man. He just doted on Judith—got her that plane and flying lessons, outfitted her vet clinic with all the latest equipment. The only thing they disagreed on was the motel. She hates it, hates the zoo, hates living there. But he loved it all. Couldn't see how it was never going to turn into the fancy resort he dreamed it could be."

Behind Harriet, Lucy waved at Nick to keep the conversation going. He felt like he was grasping at straws as he said, "And it was one of his own snakes that bit him?"

"He was the only one who'd go near those snakes. He didn't even let Judith touch them. I don't see the appeal, myself. We got enough snakes to worry about around here without putting them on display."

Nick remembered the question that had snagged his curiosity earlier back at the motel. "But I noticed he didn't have any local snakes. You guys have several varieties of rattlesnakes, but he didn't keep any in his collection."

"Really? I never thought of that. I guess you're right. But he didn't actually collect any of those snakes. Not by himself. He bought them online. I know because I had to sign for them when they arrived, being postmistress and all."

"This might sound funny, but you wouldn't happen to have those records? Could I maybe get a look?"

"Why? You think someone sent him the wrong snake?"

"Something like that."

"But it was so long ago, and they're all dead. What does it matter?"

Nick gave her his most charming smile. "Guess it doesn't. I was just curious, is all."

She shrugged. "I got nothing else to do, with everyone gone on the search. It's all computer nowadays, so let me see." She tapped a few keys and looked up. "Hey, that was easier than I thought. Here you go. Seven snakes, all accounted for."

Nick pivoted to see the screen, holding his phone to grab a few quick shots of it. The snakes were listed by their scientific genus and species; he'd need to look them up to find their common names. When he was a kid, he'd briefly been interested in snakes, until a near-miss encounter with a timber rattler had squelched his curiosity. But none of these names looked familiar.

Lucy returned from Bill's office, holding a photo of him in his sheriff's uniform. "Is it okay if we take this?"

"Sure." Harriet looked from Lucy to Nick, suspicion narrowing her eyes. "You're taking that to Deena?"

"If she needs it. Let's hope it doesn't come to that." Lucy turned to the map, her finger tracing the quadrants south and west of the search perimeter. "How come some of these areas have a sticky note on them? Does that mean they've been cleared even though the search has shifted to the east?"

Harriet stepped forward and squinted at the areas. "I didn't put those up. Must've been Gleason or one of the team leaders. I guess maybe folks covered those before Bill sent that text."

"Is there anything interesting in those sectors?"

"Same as anywhere else around here. A few good huckleberry picking sites is all I can think of."

Lucy frowned at that, doubtful.

Nick took Lucy's arm and led her to the door. "Thanks, Harriet. You're a gem."

"I don't know what you two are up to, but if it finds Bill, I'm glad to have helped." The phone rang again, but before she answered it, she said, "Just don't go running off anywhere without calling in to me first. The last thing we need around here is two more city slickers lost."

CHAPTER 25

LUCY AND NICK WALKED BACK to where they'd parked Bill's truck. "What did you find?" Nick asked her, once he had climbed into the passenger seat.

"Nothing. I guess he kept everything at home or with him in the Jeep."

"Where to next?"

"The only person who seems willing to talk about what Bill was looking into is Gus Holmstead." She put the truck in gear. "Plus I want to ask him about those geological engineers. There's something off about them."

"Let's go."

Lucy drove them east out of town to the Magruder Corridor. She turned down the drive onto the Holmstead land, this time following it all the way instead of turning off to head into the forest. On the way she told Nick about her morning: the bear trap, the engineers' camp, and her conversation with Gus.

Finally, she slowed to a stop in front of the Holmstead home. There were no other vehicles visible and no sign of Amy or Gus. She climbed out of the truck, waiting for Nick to join her.

"What's wrong?" he asked.

"I don't know." She didn't even realize it when her hand skimmed beneath her tee to settle on the Beretta holstered at the small of her back, it was such an automatic reflex. But a reflex triggered by what? "Something feels off."

A curtain rustled in an open window on the second floor. Except...the wind was coming from the other direction.

"Back in the truck," she ordered Nick. To his credit, he trusted her instincts enough that he moved without questioning her or hesitating. She stepped back, the truck's engine block providing cover from the house. If Gus or Amy were inside, they would have heard the truck arriving and have come to greet them.

She was debating her options when a shout sounded from inside. "Help!" a woman's voice called. Before Lucy could react, a shot was fired from the second floor window.

Lucy drew and returned fire. She jumped into the pickup's cab where Nick had crouched low. Another shot, this one pinging off the truck's bed. She started it and peeled away, dust billowing in their wake as two more shots sounded.

A glance in the rearview revealed a SUV careening around the barn, barreling straight at them and cutting off any chance of escaping to the main road.

"What about Amy and Gus?" Nick asked. "We need to go back. We're headed the wrong way."

"That was Amy screaming. I don't know where Gus is." Or even if he was still alive, she thought. One hostage was much less work than two for the same amount of leverage. "Can you get a call out?"

Nick already had his cell in his hand, trying. They had reached the narrow lane between the fenced-in pastures, tall grass whipping in the wind. The llamas, horses, goats, and alpacas all watched the two human vehicles race past, bumping along the rutted gravel drive.

"No service," Nick reported. He leaned out his window, peering at the side view mirror. "That's Davenport riding shotgun. Another guy is driving, I can't see." He pulled his head back inside the truck. "He's got a gun. Why would an engineer need a gun? Why would they be shooting at us or want to hurt Gus and Amy?"

"It's my fault. I must have spooked them this morning when we showed up at their camp."

"Yeah, but what do they want? Do you think they have anything to do with Bill?"

Lucy had no answers, so she focused on driving. There was no room to maneuver; they were penned in by wire and fence posts. Ahead they would re-enter the forest where the road grew even more rugged and constrained. She glanced across the meadow to their right. It had the most room to maneuver, and beyond it lay the gully with the dry creek bed she and Gleason had driven on this morning when he cut down it to the river. If she could find a place where the bank wasn't too steep or covered with rocks and boulders, they could follow the creek bed, reversing the route from this morning, cut over to the main drive, circle back around to the house, and help Gus and Amy.

Or follow the track the whole way to the main road, get help, and then return. Either way, at least they had options other than being herded straight into the river on the other side of the forest.

"Hold on," she told Nick, as she fastened her seatbelt, glanced to make sure he had his on, and then spun the wheel and aimed the truck between two fence posts.

The wire twanged and rattled over the truck's hood and windshield before finally snapping as she accelerated across the uneven ground. Both fence posts came out of their anchor holes, bouncing behind the truck and right into Davenport's SUV as it turned to follow them. Score one for the good guys, Lucy thought as she fought to keep the truck from spinning out on the slick grass. The ground was disappearing quickly; she had to make a decision about where to enter the gully.

The SUV was gaining on them again—and now was on a tangent that would prevent Lucy from turning toward the main drive, effectively herding them toward the river.

"Try again," she told Nick.

"Still can't get through—there's no signal."

"There was earlier. They must have cut the satellite service." That meant at least one of the four men had to be at the house still. Two in the SUV. So at most one left at the river camp. Maybe going that direction wouldn't be the worst option.

But first she had to stop Davenport and his partner in the SUV. She spotted a row of boulders lining the edge of the gully ahead.

"Take the wheel," she told Nick, as she slowed just enough to allow the SUV to draw even with them. She kept her foot firmly on the gas while Nick steered. She raised her Beretta, aiming for the SUV. Fancy shots like hitting the tires only happened in the movies; she was fine with simply distracting them.

She fired three shots, all hitting the SUV's sidewall and doors—nothing lethal, not at this range, but enough to draw the driver's attention, so that he steered toward her, trying to give Davenport a better shot. Lucy yanked the wheel back from Nick while hitting the brakes, spinning into a donut over the grass. The SUV flew past, Davenport's shots missing them, but it was going too fast and had no room to maneuver before it hit the boulders and launched into the air over the gully.

Lucy was also out of room, but she'd slowed the pickup and was able to skid past the boulders before hurtling over the edge and into the creek bed. The pickup was airborne for a gut-clenching second and almost came close to breaching the gully altogether and landing on the opposite side. But then they were dropping, pitching nose first.

A crash sounded from upstream, but Lucy had no time to register it. In the side view mirror, she saw the SUV rolling over and spinning across the creek bed. Then the gully's far side filled her vision and they rammed the rock wall.

The truck plowed through the mud and layer of loose gravel to hit solid bedrock. The driver side airbag blew out, blinding Lucy for a long moment. Gravity shifted, yanking her forward against her seatbelt then down as the pickup's momentum propelled the truck bed up and over, flipping it nose down into the creek bed. Lucy and Nick were tossed around, but the engine block took the brunt of the damage.

The truck shimmied and came to a stop with a groan of metal. Lucy blinked against the smoke from the airbag. The front windshield was cracked and caved in, and they were facing the creek bed, tilted at an oblique angle, the truck not quite all the way flipped over. She felt aches and bruises already sprouting but nothing major. Thankfully she'd let go of the wheel at the last minute; otherwise the air bag probably would have broken her wrist. Somehow she'd managed to hang onto her Beretta. "Nick?"

She braced herself on the steering wheel—which was now oriented down—and turned. Nick's side had no airbag. He'd slammed his head against the dash, and blood seeping from where he lay face down.

"Nick?" she shouted, her ears ringing.

Her door wouldn't budge but her window had been open, so she undid her seatbelt and hoisted herself out. Upstream the SUV lay on its side, wedged in by a bottleneck in the gully walls. No one had emerged from it yet.

Lucy stumbled around to Nick's side of the truck. The force of the impact had popped his door open. He was breathing, moaning, and finally raised his head. "Wait, don't move. Does your neck hurt? Can you feel everything?"

Blood was dripping down his face, and there was already a lump forming on his forehead. She checked his neck and did a quick scan for any serious injuries.

"Cracked a few ribs," he muttered, wincing when she ran her hands over his right side. "But it's my leg—I felt something snap."

She crouched low. His right leg had gotten caught between the truck's frame and the metal seat support. "Okay, pull your weight up off the seat, and I'm going to slide it out." A horn went off in the distance—Davenport and his partner were stirring. "C'mon, we need to hurry."

He hoisted himself up, climbing up along the tilted dash, and she guided his ankle and foot free. Then he leaned his weight against her as he climbed out. A grunt of pain escaped him when he tried to put weight on his ankle. He hobbled a few steps, one arm draped around her shoulder, but then she spotted a glint of metal. Her walking stick—it had been sitting beneath the dash on Nick's side of the truck and had fallen out when the door flew open.

"Use this." She handed him the stick, and he took a few experimental steps, wincing with pain. "Keep going. I'll get our packs."

Both their daypacks had been tossed into the rear compartment behind the seats. She'd have to climb all the way into the truck to reach them. Before she made it even to the open door of the truck, shots rang out.

She ducked down. Neither Davenport nor his partner had gotten free of their SUV, but Davenport had pulled his torso and arms out of the passenger side window to shoot at them. His shots went wild—no wonder, given his awkward position. He was just trying to slow them down, which was the last thing Lucy was about to do.

She abandoned the packs and ran back to Nick. "Go, go, go. He can't hit us, but they're going to get clear of that wreck soon. Or his friends will hear the noise and come to help."

Nick kept hobbling, dodging the rocks that lined the creek bed, his long legs striding along in a strange loping-hop-limp as he coordinated the walking stick with his other leg to protect his ankle. His face was red not just with blood but with pain, his lips so tight they were almost white.

This was no good. If they kept going down the wash, they'd end up at Davenport's camp—and there might be company waiting for them there. Plus the loose dirt of the creek bed was great for footprints, creating a track a blind man could see. They needed cover, a place to hide—and a way to call for help.

Lucy dug in her pocket and pulled out Gleason's bear trap map. She knew just the place. All they had to do was get there before Davenport or his friends caught up to them.

Chapter 26

Lucy helped Nick climb out of the wash, then took a few seconds to lay a false trail continuing toward the river and climbing out on the opposite side. Finally she made her way back to where Nick had taken cover behind some small bushes and saplings.

"You have a plan?" he panted.

She handed him the map, mainly to distract him. "We're about here." She pointed. They were almost midway between Gleason's two bear traps. "The house is here."

She knelt at his foot, gingerly unlacing his boot. Then she quickly removed her own left boot and her AFO brace. The rigid plastic made for a perfect splint.

"I'm not sure I can make it all the way back to the house," Nick admitted.

"It's okay. I know someplace closer." From the map, the terrain between here and the bear trap Gleason had showed her this morning was relatively flat. And it was closer than the Holmstead house. She'd get Nick there where he'd be safe and could use the trap's Wi-Fi to call for help while she went to the house and checked on Gus and Amy.

It wasn't much of a plan, not against four men with semi-automatic rifles and who knew what other weapons, but it was a start.

"This is going to hurt, but I need you to keep quiet." Even though they couldn't be seen from the creek bed, sound carried.

Nick nodded and clenched his jaw and fists, and she tugged his boot off. His ankle and foot were already swollen, but his pulse was good. There was an angry red gouge above his boot where the metal had impacted. She fastened her AFO around his ankle, tightening it to give him as much support as possible, and carefully slid his foot back into his boot. That was the tough part, but no way could he travel barefoot. She felt his entire body go rigid with pain, so she moved as fast as she could. And then it was done.

"We've got to go." She handed him her walking stick, pulled his free arm and most of his weight onto her shoulders, squatted, and together they got him back on his feet. "Can you walk?"

"Lead the way," he said through gritted teeth. She took a moment to wipe the blood from his face with her sleeve and gave him a quick kiss.

"We can do this," she promised him. He gave her a weak smile that said he was trying to believe her.

The important thing was to put as much distance between them and Davenport as fast as possible. Another reason she'd chosen the bear trap. Because of the way the roads and the creek bed curved, their trail overland was almost perpendicular to the path Davenport would take if he followed the road.

That didn't make it easy, though. Their

path grew steep, the foliage so thick that they both tripped and stumbled several times, but they were able to catch each other before anyone could fall. Lucy kept her right arm wrapped around Nick, her Beretta in her left. She had five bullets left, plus her second Beretta in her ankle holster had another ten.

Since they'd lost their packs, they had no food or water or equipment other than what was on them. Which came down to two folding knives, two pistols, one cell phone—Nick's was in his pocket but she'd left hers on the charger in Bill's truck—a notepad, a permanent marker, one tiny MagLite, a compass, two bandanas, and a small roll of duct tape.

Once they'd placed some distance between them and Davenport, Lucy used one of the bandanas as a pressure dressing on Nick's scalp wound, securing it with a strip of duct tape.

"Just a little bit farther."

Nick wasn't doing much talking, saving his energy. He simply nodded, pushed off the boulder he'd been sitting on with the walking stick, and continued to trudge along the narrow game trail they'd been following.

They climbed up a small hill, and she saw the blind canyon with the waterfall at its far end. "That's it." She motioned to Nick to wait while she scouted the area. Once they went down to the trap, they were committed; there was only one path out. And she couldn't help but remember the wolf tracks they'd seen that morning.

Nick finally realized the bear trap was their destination. "In there? Are you crazy?"

"It's secure. You'll be safe." She glanced up at the sun—down in the ravine like this, they were already losing light fast, even though it was a few hours before official sunset. Gleason had said he'd be coming to shut down the other bear trap sometime this afternoon. Would he stop by this one again?

She glanced around searching for one of Gleason's trail cameras—she needed to warn him. Otherwise he'd be walking right into Davenport and his men.

Then she froze. There was movement on

the ridge opposite. Not human; a wolf. The silver alpha.

Nick spotted it as well. “Lucy, this is too dangerous. We need to find another way.”

“We just need to get to the trap.”

“How?”

She was working on that. Trying to remember what little she knew of wolves and pack animals. Thank goodness Megan had gone through a phase where she’d only been interested in the animal documentaries on NatGeo and Animal Planet.

“Is that a satellite on top of the bear cage?” Nick asked.

“Yes, they have Wi-Fi, and a webcam inside.” Maybe they were already close enough to use it. “I lost my phone. Let’s try yours.”

He unbuttoned his shirt pocket, winced, and pulled out a mangled block of shattered glass and bent metal. “When I hit the dash.”

“Try it anyway, maybe it’s just the screen.”

He flipped it over—the dent went through to the back and had partially popped the battery out. Gingerly, he tried to replace the it. When he had to stop to wipe the blood oozing from his scalp into his eyes, Lucy took over. Shards of glass broke free from the screen as she tried to reshape the phone back to its normal configuration. She was able to straighten it enough that she got the battery into place, but no matter what she did, she couldn't get the phone to power on. "It's dead."

"The webcam in the trap," Nick said, obviously warming to her plan. "We can alert Gleason. He'll bring help."

But the wolves. They had to get past them first. Then she could worry about predators on two feet. On the video Gleason had shown them earlier, the wolves had come from all directions, but their main fighting force had attacked from up on the ridge, taking advantage of the higher ground.

She peered at the area around the trap. There was no sign of any other wolves. Maybe the alpha was alone? On a scouting mission?

The wolf hadn't moved, and was still staring at them—at her, it felt like—from across the ravine. As Lucy watched, it dipped his head as if nodding, making a promise. And then it vanished.

"Now," she urged Nick.

They scrambled down the side of the ravine, bracing themselves with hands, feet, whatever they could find. Lucy's ankle protested, but she ignored it. With each step, doubt overwhelmed her. What did she know about wolves? How reliable was the webcam in the trap?

They reached the trap. Lucy used the button Gleason had shown her to raise the heavy door and hoisted Nick inside. She scribbled a note warning to Gleason. "Hold this up to the camera after I close the door."

"Wait—you're coming inside as well. Lucy, I'm not staying here without you."

"The camera is only activated when the door is shut. I need to stay out here to open it again." It was a lie. Lucy had no intention staying there. She had prey of her own to hunt. She lowered the door, and it fell so fast Nick had to jump back. The sound of the metal on metal clang echoed through the woods, alien and intrusive.

"Is the camera working?" she asked, hating that their lives depended on a single piece of technology. Not just theirs—Gus's, Amy's, and Gleason's as well.

"Yeah, the light came on. I'm holding the note up. There's not much light in here, though."

"Here." She pushed her tiny MagLite through one of the air holes. She watched Nick through it. She should just leave. Now. While she knew he was safe. Maybe Davenport would never find him; maybe she didn't have to worry. But all she could envision was Davenport and his men taking potshots through the air holes in the bear trap—talk about fish in a barrel.

"Lucy, it's done. Now open the door and come inside."

Still she hesitated.

"Wait. You said *you'll* be safe." Nick finally caught up with an argument she'd already won five minutes ago. Not at all like him. Concussion—one more thing to worry about. "You meant *we*, right? We'll be safe in the bear trap. We will be safe. Together."

"They'll come at night."

"The wolves?"

God, she hoped not. Maybe they'd get lucky and the wolves wouldn't be interested in two puny injured humans reeking of adrenaline and blood. Maybe the wolves around here only liked big, strong targets like bears.

"The men. At least one of them has a rifle with a thermal scope. So one or more with night vision capabilities. Darkness isn't going to stop them hunting us."

Movement on the hill to the east caught her eye. A glint of silver among the green bushes. The alpha had returned. Right. No time left.

But then she spotted a rustling in brush on the other side of the ravine, back the way she and Nick had come. Damn—they were trying to outflank them, like they had the bear.

Black and gray and brown shadows rippled across both sides of the ravine as the wolves gathered. The blood. They smelled

Nick's blood. Once they were inside the trap, would the wolves tire of the wait and leave? She remembered what Gleason had said about the patience of wolves, how even if a moose or elk made it to relative safety in deep water, the wolves would take turns harassing their prey until the larger animal succumbed to exhaustion.

Except Lucy wasn't worried about exhaustion. She was more worried about being trapped by one predator only to give the more dangerous humans time to catch up to them. But she'd run out of time, and her hesitation may have damned them both.

She hit the switch to open the trap's door and climbed in.

"About time you came to your senses," Nick told her.

She ignored him, grabbing the walking stick and pressing the button that would collapse it to an eight-inch cylinder. "Wedge this under the door when it comes down."

Without waiting for an answer, she crawled to the rear of the culvert where the bait would hang from a lever. She looked back. Nick had the walking stick braced at the door. She yanked on the lever, triggering the trap.

CHAPTER 27

AS SOON AS THE TRAP DOOR hit the walking stick it stopped. Nick wasn't sure how the safety mechanism worked, but he was happy it did—Lucy wasn't claustrophobic, but she'd go nuts if she was trapped with no way out. Not that that excused her for even thinking of abandoning him here and heading off into danger.

"Any sign that Gleason got the message?" she asked Nick as she leaned down and peered through the narrow gap below the trap door.

"No idea," Nick answered. He sounded pissed off and knew it, but he didn't apologize—from the stiffening of her shoulders, Lucy had heard the emotion in his voice.

"The wolves are gone. Maybe the noise of the trap door clanging scared them off?"

Nick could only hope it hadn't carried far enough to invite human predators.

"I wish I understood why this was all happening," Lucy continued, as she spun around the narrow space to sit beside him, between him and the door. "I thought maybe Davenport had found the buried gold Gus told me about, but then why target Bill? Plus, Davenport didn't even get here until a day after Bill went missing. And if his men who were here first found the gold, why bring the GPR unit? Why not just dig for it?" He could barely make out her features in the dim light. She touched his hand, and he pulled his away. "Nothing makes sense."

Did she really expect him to sit here in a freakin' stinkin' bear trap and discuss the intricacies of her freakin' stinkin' case?

"We're sitting in a bear trap, surrounded by wolves—real life wolves, wolves who have no compunction against going after grizzly bears—being hunted by men with guns, and you're worried about not understanding exactly what motivated our friendly neighborhood psychopathic killers?" Nick couldn't help his laugh; it was either that or break down altogether. Because he didn't see a way out of this, not with both of them still alive. Given that he couldn't move fast or fight, given who Lucy was, he knew she had a plan, one that might save his life but would probably end up with her dead.

"Shhh...the wolves will hear you. Besides, I get Davenport's motivation—greed. I just don't understand anything else."

"Great time for an existential crisis," he snapped.

Lucy turned and pressed her lips to his. He responded to her touch—how could he not?—but her cavalier attitude only cemented his dread.

"You're getting ready to do something stupid, aren't you?" he asked, when they finally parted.

She sat quiet, thinking. She took a long time before answering, and when she did, she surprised him by talking not about the case but instead about what they'd been tiptoeing around for months.

"Existential crisis. That's a good name for it. I feel like all my life I've been defined by my job. It sure as hell defined our marriage: where we lived, what jobs you could take knowing that you might not be there more than a few years before the Bureau reassigned me. It even defined how we raised Megan: teaching her gun safety and then how to shoot and how to defend herself so she wouldn't be scared when I was gone—what did she call it?"

"Chasing the Death Eaters. Blame that one on your mom for letting her watch Harry Potter movies when she was way too young. I told her to stick to the books. She was up for weeks with nightmares."

"And I wasn't there. I was down in Alabama negotiating that hostage situation at the prison."

"I never resented your job, Lucy."

"Sure you did. Megan did when we moved from Virginia to Pittsburgh."

"But now she loves it," he interrupted

her.

"And you were so patient with the hours and crazy assignments that sent me far from home. But something changed after we moved. You changed—the way you saw me, and my job. You were glad when I left the Bureau—were you tired of being controlled by them, by my assignments?"

If they weren't being held captive by steel walls and a pack of wild wolves—yeah, he was man enough to admit it, the wolves were freaking him out even if it was much more likely that the men with guns would be the ones to kill them—if they were having this conversation anywhere else, this was when Nick would have walked away. Let things simmer and die down, hopefully to never be spoken of again. Usually he didn't avoid tough topics—Lord knew, Lucy never did until recently—but this one, this could break them if things went wrong.

"I supported your decision to leave," he began in a cautious tone.

"It wasn't really my decision, and you know it. But that's not what I'm talking about.

Even before then, before the dog and my mom—" Her voice broke, and he wrapped his arms around her, leaning his back against the curved steel wall to make room to draw her closer.

"Lucy. We don't need to talk about this. Not now."

She shook her head, her hair brushing against his face in the near-darkness. "Yes, now. Because I never meant to put you and Megan second—but I know you feel that way. That my job came first, that I was willing to risk my life for a job when I could be home with the people I love."

"I don't—" He stopped. His throat tightened, choking his words to dust. Because if he was honest with himself, he *had* felt that way; she was right about the anger and resentment at the way she so easily put herself in the line of fire for total strangers. When the FBI had forced her to leave, he'd felt relief, but now this new job... "Okay, I do. Maybe. Sometimes. But I also know that's what makes you the woman I love. That need to run toward danger while the rest of us are running away." He kissed the top of her head, wished he could see her face. "Sometimes it's just hard being married to a freakin' superhero. Being the one always left behind."

"I'm no superhero. Not even a regular hero." Her shoulders tightened against his chest, but then a chuckle rippled through her body and into his. "Bet you wished I'd left you behind this time."

"Yeah, can't blame your job for this one." He hugged her tight, his palm pressing against her heart, relishing its sure and steady beat. Unlike his own pulse, spiked by fear and adrenaline. "But there's no place else I'd rather be. No one else I'd rather be with."

"We need to think of Megan."

"I know." It was the only reason he hadn't continued to argue with her once he realized what her plan was. "But you need to know none of this is your fault."

"See? That's exactly my point. I used to blame my job. But now...it's not the job. It's me. It's who I am, and I don't know how to change or stop or—"

"Or what? Sit behind a desk pushing papers while you send others to put themselves in danger? Other people who might not do the job as well as you can? Who might get themselves hurt or someone else hurt because you're not there?" He didn't mean to sound clinical, but habit had him dropping into a neutral tone designed to allow clients to reflect on their words. He felt her breath rise through her chest and then empty out again.

"Hubris," she finally answered. "Isn't that what always brought down the wrath of gods in all those Greek tragedies? My need to control—that so-called magical thinking—it controls me, doesn't it? It's a no-win situation. Either I lead from the front, putting myself at risk to protect my team, or I send them out in my place, risking their lives, and face the consequences if things go wrong." She squirmed off his lap, swinging her legs around so she could face him in the narrow space. "Either way, you and Megan lose because you're left to pick up the pieces. That's what's been killing me. I don't know how to find a solution that doesn't hurt you two."

"I don't have the answers, but I do know that talking about it is a good first step."

She leaned her forehead against his. Close enough that even in the dim light he could see her eyes, dark and serious as they searched out his. "That's a promise. If we make it out of here, we're going to keep talking. Together. Me, you, and Megan—she deserves to be a part of this."

"Deal." Before he could say more, her lips were on his again. This time her kiss wasn't playful or the result of adrenaline; rather it was soul-shaking and more than a little terrifying. As if, despite her words promising them a future, her body was saying goodbye.

Then she pulled away, leaning against the opposite side of the trap, so far away that she appeared as only a ghostly glow in the waning sunlight.

"Let's focus on how we're going to get out of here."

He winced at her businesslike tone. But

he also understood that if she was going to survive what came next, she had to keep her emotions out of it.

She pulled her gun out, dropped the magazine, counted the bullets, replaced the magazine, pulled back the slide, and handed it to him. "The safety's off and there's a round in the chamber. Five bullets total."

He didn't argue the point, but wrapped his fingers around the Beretta, taking care to keep from touching the trigger. He was a decent shot on the range but had never had to shoot at a living creature. Hopefully tonight wouldn't break that winning streak. "How long before Gleason gets the alarm that the trap was activated?"

"I'm not sure—I guess it depends on where he is." She clamped her tiny Maglite between her teeth and scribbled another note then tore it from her notepad. "He should've gotten a text message when the camera above the door went live. But here's another—show it along with the first one once the camera goes live again." She placed the slip of paper in his free hand and wrapped his fingers around it, squeezing them tight.

"What's it say?" The first note had warned Gleason about Davenport and his men.

"Just that I'll be out there along with Davenport. And to not go to the Holmstead house himself, but to send the police, so he won't be walking into a trap."

Unlike Lucy. Who was not only walking into a trap, she was putting herself out as bait to draw attention away from Nick. He shoved the note into his pocket. Lucy edged her way to the door, peering out into the twilight. Anger and frustration swamped him. He grabbed her arm and pulled her back with an urgency that surprised them both, her eyes going wide.

He knew the rational thing was to let her go, let her remain divorced from emotions that might cloud her judgment. But to hell with rational, logical thinking. He needed her; refused to accept the possibility of a life without her in it.

"Promise me," he urged her, their bodies pressed together. "Promise me you're not going to do anything stupid, that you're going to play it safe. Promise me you're going to make it back." It was the one thing she prided herself on, never making a promise she couldn't keep. "I need to hear the words. Lucy, promise me."

"Now who's putting their faith in magical thinking?" she chided him, even as her fingers stroked his cheek. "Nothing I say, no words, will make a difference."

"They will to me. Promise me."

He hated her hesitation. In those few seconds lay the destruction of all their hopes and dreams. Not just his and Lucy's, Megan's as well. Finally, she raised her chin as if defying every god in heaven, looked him in the eye, and said, "I promise."

And then she was gone. She removed the walking stick and the trap door lowered, cutting off what little light he had, leaving Nick alone in the dark.

Chapter 28

WITH THE HELP OF THE WALKING STICK, Lucy climbed to the top of the ridge, aiming for the path that led to the Holmstead house. Once off the scree with its shifting ground, she felt more secure and was able to move fairly silently, if slowly, through the forest. She sensed animals moving but couldn't see or hear them. Nothing seemed to be coming close—if anything, they were headed away from the ravine and the bear trap. Then she heard the distant growl of an ATV coming up the trail Gleason had used this morning. No, make that two all-terrain vehicles coming from the direction of the house. Davenport and his men.

At most she could expect four bad guys.

Three, if Amy and Gus were still alive and one had been left to guard them. But best to count on four. If she took care of them, she could deal with everything else.

The trick would be to get them to reveal themselves, then for her to get close enough to take them out one by one, using the Beretta as the last resort—the sound and muzzle flare would give her position away.

No food, no water, no ankle brace to support her leg on this rugged terrain, no jacket, no Kevlar, no backup...at least none coming anytime soon. It would depend on when Gleason received Nick's message and how long it took him to get here. She reassessed her assets. In addition to her Beretta and folding knife, she had what was left of the roll of duct tape, the map of the bear traps that Gleason had given her, her MagLite and walking stick, belt, holster...oh! She wore it every day; how could she have forgotten? The bracelet Megan had given her—it was made of woven paracord. Perfect.

She released the bracelet's plastic clasp

and pocketed the handcuff key secreted within—Megan had initially added it as a joke, but that handcuff key had saved Lucy's life back in January—and unwound the black paracord. For some reason, clutching the length of thin rope in her hand she felt stronger, more confident about the outcome.

True, the bad guys were fighting over a priceless treasure and maybe also trying to get away with murder, but Lucy was fighting for something so much more precious: her family.

Davenport and his men didn't stand a chance.

First, she needed to lead them away from Nick. No; first she'd set her traps. Then draw them in before they reached Nick.

She scrambled down the forested side of the hill and staked out a chokepoint where the trail narrowed and she found two trees just the right distance apart. She tied the paracord at neck height, stretching it taut. The black cord was invisible in the darkness. Then she found a place for her ambush—a slight rise in the trail just before the choke point. She bent a long, flexible branch down, fastened her belt around it, then anchored the belt with a rock on the side of the trail. She could just make out her belt buckle glistening in the faint moonlight.

Then she sidled silently down the trail until she reached a sharp curve. Once she rounded it, she jogged as fast as she could, heading directly behind the path of the ATVs that, from the noise, weren't far away at all.

When she grew close to the ATVs, she turned her MagLite on and used it to light her way, purposefully waving it so they'd see someone there but not well enough to aim accurately. She hoped.

Finally, one of the men spotted her light reflecting from the treetops and shouted to his companions. The ATVs slowed to a stop. Lucy could see the men turning toward her, their faces pale in the dim light. The ATV closest to her held two men. Lucy aimed her light directly into the passenger's eyes as he turned around in his seat and raised his weapon. Then she spun, turned off her light, and raced back down the trail. The whine of the ATVs gunning their engines as they turned around on the narrow trail to follow her filled the night sky.

Her bad ankle almost tripped her up—without the brace, her toes tended to drag on the ground—but the walking stick kept her upright, and she managed to reach her belt just as the ATVs sped around the curve. She tugged on the belt, releasing the tree limb so that it sprang back hard enough to rustle the brush while she dove into her ambush site on the other side of the path.

She drew her pistol and waited, quieting her breathing.

"Where'd she go?" A man's voice sounded over the noise of the ATVs.

"There's movement in the trees."

"Cut her off!"

The first ATV, the one carrying two men, sped up while the second slowed and its driver fired his AR-15 into the shuddering bushes across from where Lucy lay in wait. Then came the scream of a man as the first ATV's driver was caught by her paracord clothesline.

Lucy came up beside the second ATV,

whose driver was now facing away from her as he aimed into the trees. "Drop it," she told him.

He started to lower his rifle but the third man, who'd been riding behind the driver on the lead ATV, appeared in her periphery. Before she could do anything, he began to fire. He had his semi-automatic rifle on burst and let loose a volley of shots in rapid succession, all hitting wide of the mark as he lost control, going wide and high.

Lucy dove, using the ATV for cover and the muzzle flash to target the shooter. The man above her cried out as the flurry of bullets ripped through him and fell forward, motionless.

She fired at the shooter. Two quick shots, center mass. He grunted in pain, dropping his weapon as he slumped to the ground. Cautiously, she crept toward the stalled lead ATV. Its driver was nowhere to be seen—the clothesline maneuver may have stunned him, but it clearly hadn't incapacitated him.

She turned back to the man on the dirt between the two ATVs. He had the AR-15 with the thermal imaging scope. He was still breathing but in short gasps, blowing blood-tinged bubbles with each breath. She took his rifle, but before she could raise it to sight through the scope, a burst of gunfire from the trees beyond her drove her back behind the ATV for cover. Damn, the last man must also have night vision capacity. And he was a much better shot than his partner. There was a rustle of bushes as he left the trail, taking cover himself.

The all-terrain vehicle was low to the ground, but Lucy was skinny enough to belly crawl under it. She sighted into the bushes with the rifle, searching for a heat signature—while hoping that the ATV's engine would help to conceal hers. Nothing, nothing, nothing... He couldn't be moving, she'd see that, so he must also be behind cover. She chose the largest tree, the one she'd choose if she was searching for cover, and kept it in the center of her sights.

She was rewarded. As the engine cooled, ticking away the seconds of camouflage it could provide, the white figure of a man's heat signature emerged, sighting his rifle directly at her. She fired first. Single shots, one, two, three, all aimed center mass. He lurched back, his arms flailing up, and then fell.

Lucy crawled out from under the ATV. Her ears were ringing, making the forest seem otherworldly in its silence. She methodically checked each man. All dead. She took one dead man's magazine from his weapon and used its rounds to top off the magazine of the rifle she kept. They had satellite phones, so she called 911 and got Harriet and quickly explained the situation.

"Judith's already headed that way," Harriet told her. "She might even be at the house—she got a text alert from one of Gleason's bear traps and tried to reach him and couldn't, so she knew he'd be out there."

"Why would Judith get alerts for the traps?"

"If an animal's injured, she has to be prepared."

"Call her, tell her to find cover, stay put, and wait for backup. She could be walking into a hostage situation. There's at least one more armed man out there." Davenport hadn't been with his partners. Lucy could only hope that he had kept Gus, Amy, and Gleason alive to use as bargaining tools.

"I'll call you back." Harriet hung up.

Lucy started the ATV and began down the trail towards the Holmstead house. She wasn't intending to do more than surveil the situation and wait for backup, but then Harriet called.

"Judith isn't picking up, and it will be twenty minutes at least before I can get anyone to you—probably longer because the deputies are out ferrying search volunteers all over God's green earth."

"Call the state police, get them moving. And EMS—they can get Nick out of the bear trap. But tell them not to come anywhere near the house until the scene is clear." Lucy cut the ATV's engine as she reached the burnt out tree that marked the turnoff to the main house. She climbed off and moved as quickly and quietly as she could down the gravel path toward the house.

"What are you going to do?" Harriet asked.

Lucy was still a hundred yards out when she heard two gunshots. Damn. No time left.

"I'm going in."

Chapter 29

When Lucy drew closer to the house, she saw several vehicles now parked out front: a pickup truck and a large SUV. The house and surrounding buildings were all dark. She scanned for heat signatures, but the only ones she saw came from the engine of the pickup truck and a person inside the cab.

Keeping her pistol handy, she carefully and quietly approached the truck. It was Gleason's. The front windshield was shot out and the rear one starred with bullet holes. She reached the driver's side. The door was open, Gleason slumped over in the seat.

He was breathing, but there was blood gushing from his right chest. Lucy backed away, moving around to the passenger side. She eased the door open, thankful that there was no interior light to give her position away to anyone in the house, and crawled inside.

"Who?" Gleason moaned.

Lucy didn't answer, but instead opened the glove compartment hoping to find a first aid kit. Nothing. She crawled around her seat to search the narrow space behind the seats. Bingo—a field kit was stowed behind the driver's seat. She also spotted a blown out hole in the seat that corresponded to Gleason's wound.

"This is good," she told him in a low voice. "The bullet went all the way through. Are you having trouble breathing?"

"Just the pain. Think it cracked a rib."

A high-powered rifle, it had probably done a lot more than that. But he was talking okay, so that was a good sign.

She opened the field kit, grabbed some gauze, and packed his exit wound where most of the blood was coming from. Then she used a square of gauze still sealed in its plastic coating to create a makeshift flutter valve over the entrance wound, taping it on three sides. "This will let any air build up release. Just leave it; don't cover it."

"Amy and Gus—"

"I'm going now. You just stay tight." His radio had fallen to the cab floor. Probably a good thing since there was a base station in Gus's kitchen. She handed him her sat phone instead. "Call Harriet and keep her updated."

He nodded, clutching the phone with both hands. Lucy squeezed his arm and left. Using the two vehicles as cover, she reached the front porch. She crouched low, skirting around the house. She tried to look into the windows, but they were all over her head until she reached the bay window at the rear, which was low enough to the ground that she could peer into the kitchen.

The only light was coming from the bulb over the stove, but it was enough for her to see Davenport where he'd taken up position beside the refrigerator, its bulk protecting him from any assault from the rear of the house. He'd positioned a wall mirror over the microwave, angled so he could see all the way to the front door, enabling him to cover both sides of the house.

She ducked back down. No sign of Gus or Amy. It had to be Judith's SUV out front, but there was no sign of her either. Maybe they were all dead—but their absence gave her options. She could shoot Davenport and probably kill him, but then she'd have no answers about what had happened to Bill. Or what Davenport was after. Plus she was already responsible for three men dying tonight; no reason to add a fourth if she didn't need to.

"Drop the weapon, Davenport," she called to him, taking a position to far side of the bay window, between it and the kitchen door.

His answer was a burst of gunfire that shattered one of the large windowpanes. "You drop yours, Lucy! Otherwise Gus and Amy die."

"Talk to me—what's going on?"

"They have a radio; I heard the call for the cops and state police. So don't waste my time. All I want is a way out of here and enough time to grab what's mine."

"You mean the gold?" She was guessing, but it was the only thing that made sense. "Is that why you came after me and Nick?"

"We found it. But that girl came waltzing in on one of those damn llamas and saw us digging it up. Plus the boss stranded us down there with no way to get it out—didn't trust us. So we brought the girl up to the house to take their SUV. Stupid old man had to put up a fight and it took longer than it should've—the others wanted to just shoot 'em both, but I figured a few bargaining chips stashed away couldn't hurt. Guess I was right."

Until Lucy and Nick had come along at just the wrong time and ruined everything. Had they also gotten Gus and Amy killed?

"Are Gus and Amy okay?" Lucy asked, holding her breath for the answer.

"He and the girl are fine. For now." He raised the hand not clutching his rifle, revealing a cell phone. "But all it takes is a little det cord and a blasting cap to change that."

Had he turned the Wi-Fi back on? She

didn't have her cell phone to check to see if there was service, which meant she had to take his threat seriously. She'd seen the SWAT team blow through metal doors with a few feet of det cord—she didn't want to imagine what it could do to a human body. The only good thing was that there was no easy way to rig a dead man's switch using a cell phone. But all he needed was a split instant to press a button and send the trigger message to his IED.

She rested her rifle beside the kitchen door and kept her Beretta holstered. Her collapsed walking stick rested in the side pocket of her cargo pants. Maybe it wasn't as good as an ASP, but it could still make for an effective weapon.

"I'm coming in." All she had to do was buy enough time for backup to arrive. Or maybe give him what he wanted—given that there was only one road in or out, he was as good as caught already. She extended both hands, nudged the screen door open with her hip, and sidled inside, keeping her back to the wall. "Tell me where Gus and Amy are and I'll let you leave."

"In the basement." He trained his rifle on her. "If you're here, my guys are gone, aren't they?" He nodded to the radio base station on the desk beside the kitchen table. "I heard chatter about three being down. That was you?"

"I thought you were in a hurry to leave. Go on, no one's stopping you. But you don't have much time. You'll need to take the SUV—you shot up Gleason's truck, so I doubt it will run. But before you go, tell me where Bill Beachey is."

"What are you talking about?" He frowned, as if suspecting a trap. "What SUV?"

Before Lucy could answer, a shot cracked through the window. Davenport rocked back against the refrigerator and then slumped to the floor, his brains leaving a bloody trail on the white enamel. Lucy drew her Beretta and spun. Judith was standing at the window, holding the rifle Lucy had left behind.

Lucy ran to grab Davenport's cell. No message sent. Then she turned to Judith, who had entered the kitchen, still holding the rifle at the ready, her expression blank.

"Put the rifle down on the floor, Judith," Lucy told her in a calm, steady voice, even as she edged away from the muzzle. Slowly, Judith complied, just as the sound of approaching vehicles sounded. "Go outside and tell the others it's safe. Get help for Gleason. I'm going to check on Amy and Gus."

Judith nodded in slow motion, her eyes still fixed on Davenport's corpse. Then she turned on her heel and ran out the door, gagging like she might vomit.

Chapter 30

By the time the State Police finished with Lucy and Judith, it was well past midnight. Amy and Gus were fine, just a bit shaken after their ordeal, while Gleason and Nick were being flown by helicopter to the Harborview trauma center in Seattle, the same hospital Gleason's mother worked at.

They took her Beretta but promised to get it back to her after they were done with ballistic testing. Finally, Lucy found herself riding in Judith's SUV headed back to the motel.

"I'd offer to fly you to Seattle, but we still haven't given up on finding Bill," Judith said. "Did Davenport tell you anything helpful?"

"I asked him about Bill, but he didn't

seem to know anything. He talked about a boss, though. Made it sound as if someone had sent them after the gold. I'm guessing it's someone local—how else could four guys from North Dakota know where to look for buried treasure?"

"It definitely wasn't Gus or Amy," she answered.

"Can I borrow your phone?"

"There won't be any news on Nick or Gleason, not yet."

"I know. I just want to check in back home."

Judith shrugged. It was almost four in the morning back in Pittsburgh, but knowing Wash he'd still be up—or would already be up. Wash had a twenty-something's metabolism that refused to heed the sun's schedule. Lucy dialed his cell.

"Hello?" he answered hesitantly, probably surprised by the strange number on his caller ID.

"It's me, Lucy. Just checking in, letting you know everything's okay here."

"Any reason why it shouldn't be?" She heard computer keys clicking in the background as she shifted the phone to her right ear, the one farthest from Judith. "Oh, wow, you guys have been busy."

"I was afraid you might see something online. Nick has a broken leg; they took him to a hospital in Seattle. I'm with Judith, heading back to the motel."

"Wait. Judith Keenan? Did you get my messages about her? I've been texting and emailing—I even called your friend, and asked her to tell you to call me."

"No, sorry. I lost my phone. What happened?" She kept her tone light.

"Well, I checked those death investigations. The only names that popped were the two coroners. But when I dug deeper into Judith's, I found she has a string of deaths she's connected to, going back way to before she moved to Idaho. Two other husbands died—one from a heart attack, the other in a boating accident."

"No, don't wake Megan. What else

happened?" She smiled at Judith and made a quacking gesture with her fingers.

"Nothing that ever looked suspicious—until you start to add them up. All from different jurisdictions, going back decades. Plus she had different names because of being married more than once, so no one police department or medical examiner ever got the chance to piece things together. Including some weird shit. Like a fellow veterinary student died of a nitrous oxide overdose—making Judith valedictorian by default. And there's more."

"No worries, I'll get back to you first thing. As soon as I hear from the hospital. We're pulling up to Judith's motel now, so I need to go."

"Do you want me to send backup?"

She rolled her eyes. *Finally*. For a genius, sometimes Wash could be a bit dense. "Sure, why not?"

"Okay, but it might take them awhile. Be careful. Better yet, just get out of there and let the cops sort it all out."

"Wish I could do that. Give her a kiss for

me." Lucy hung up.

Judith took her phone back and slid it into her pocket as she pulled the SUV to a stop. She hopped out and was around to Lucy's side just as Lucy was opening the door. It swung wide to reveal Judith holding a semi-automatic pistol aimed at Lucy. "What gave it away?"

Lucy started to play along, but she was just too damned tired of people pointing guns at her—plus the gleam in Judith's eye said she wouldn't be fooled anyway. Lucy climbed down from the van, keeping her hands in plain sight. The only weapon left to her was the walking stick, now collapsed and resting in her pocket.

"Let's go," Judith told her. Together they traveled through the dimly lit reception area and down the grand hall. Judith was smart, keeping enough distance that Lucy had no chance at tackling her, but remaining close enough that there was no way she could miss Lucy if she pulled the trigger.

Finally, they ended up in the zoo. Judith had Lucy stand back against the railing above the tiger's enclosure. She reached for a large cattle prod from the collection hanging on the wall, eying Lucy, clearly making a plan. Below Lucy the tiger stirred, rolling upright from where it had been lying on a boulder, and making a low throaty noise as if protesting the human intrusion into its peaceful evening.

"It would be so very easy," Judith said. "After all, Tabby is fascinating. You lean over the enclosure barrier to get a better look, and oh my, that clumsy, weak ankle of yours gives way, and whoops! You fall inside. I, of course, think quickly and grab my trusty tranq gun, but you move into my line of fire and get the dart instead. No time to reload, so I use the electric prod—accidentally on purpose agitating Tabby with seventy-thousand volts if she hasn't already pounced. Then I single-handedly fight off the massive beast and eventually subdue her, but it's too late for poor, poor Lucy." Her grin was more tiger-like than Tabby's. "I'd be a hero. And no one would question me. They never do."

"Because you're too smart for them," Lucy said. All she needed to do was buy some time. "The good doctor, always with an answer, a story that feels more real than the unthinkable: that you're a killer. But it wasn't always that way, was it? You didn't start out to kill them, right? You just found yourself coroner in an out-of-the-way, boring county, and it was all so mundane, who could resist making things a bit more exciting? Changing a lab result there—or never running the labs, just forging them. Maybe you thought you were saving the county money or the families some grief, giving them something unique about their loved ones' deaths, a special story to hang on to."

"Wrong, wrong, wrong." Judith laughed. "You're not as smart as you think you are. I started doing this back in high school. My first boyfriend—he was damn lucky to have me, but he was too depressed, sunken into his emo-funk, constantly whining to me about how miserable his life was, that he should just end it all. I couldn't take it any more, so I put him out of his misery."

"You killed him?" In high school? Lucy quickly reassessed the threat Judith posed.

"No. Where'd the fun be in that? It would be over much too quickly. I spent weeks working on him, convincing him to go through with it, until finally he did it—he hung himself. Then I got to play the grief-stricken girlfriend, getting all that attention while getting away with murder." Her eyes gleamed with excitement. "It was intoxicating. Knowing I was smarter than everyone, playing the kind-hearted bumbling fat girl while all along I was manipulating them to do whatever I damned well wanted."

"But eventually you did begin to kill. Hands on." All those strange deaths littering Judith's past; they weren't coincidence.

"Not everyone is as accommodating as my boyfriend. Or stupid. But I'm not afraid of death. When I was a kid growing up in Kentucky, it was animals—anyone competing with me in 4-H, I'd sneak a little antifreeze into their animal's water. But our leader got suspicious and came to talk to my mother, told her maybe I needed help. She laughed in his face. And on the way home, driving over the ice and snow, he passed out at the wheel and spun into a tree at full speed."

Lucy assumed a look of awe; Judith's ego was easy to feed. "How'd you do it? You were just a kid, right?"

"Not me. Mom. She spiked his coffee with Gramps' diabetes pills. The same way she got rid of Gramps when his pension checks stopped coming. Told me to never suffer fools." She gestured with the gun, pushing Lucy back against the railing above the tiger enclosure. "I know what you're trying to get me to do, but I don't mind. It's nice to have someone I can talk to about all this. Especially as I know no one's coming to help you and you'll never be able to tell anyone."

"Where's Bill?"

Judith shook her head. "Gone."

"Did you tell him everything before you killed him?"

"I couldn't risk it. He's so much bigger and stronger than me, I had to take him by surprise. Although I admit, he surprised me first. He was asking the right questions, just of the wrong person. He came so close; I wish I knew how. Did he tell you? Is that how you caught on to me?"

"No, he never said anything about you. He never mentioned you at all. Other than as the poor woman whose husband died after dragging her out of her big city job and all the way up here." If Lucy was hoping that the blow to Judith's ego would rattle the other woman, she was mistaken—Judith actually smirked at the news that Bill had never suspected her.

"Then how did you find me?" She sounded eager for career advice so she wouldn't make the same mistake twice.

Lucy was happy to oblige. Anything to keep her talking.

"We were so focused on looking for a missing person who was wandering lost or perhaps who'd harmed themselves that I never asked the most basic questions of any investigation. Why? Why this victim? Why now? Why here? Or, I should say, why anywhere but here."

"And did you find any answers?"

"Theories. Why Bill? First I thought it

was because he'd made a hobby of re-examining death investigations."

"Right. His serial killer theory. He told me about it, and asked me to review a few cases that Dr. Carruthers handled over in Idaho County." She chuckled as if at a private joke.

"Yeah, I'll bet you loved that. Because you were setting Carruthers up, weren't you? He'd done something to piss you off, and you were going to make him look like a fool in return."

"He couldn't stand that I had no formal medical training. He was always was so superior and condescending when we spoke, reminding me constantly that he wouldn't expect a veterinarian to understand. So, yeah, I had a little fun at his expense. Nothing anyone can prove—which is why I didn't mind Bill taking a look."

"Right. That had me headed in the wrong direction for a while. But then I realized the key was in the *where*, not the why. Or better yet, the where you wanted us *not* to look. Because you found a clue to where the gold was, didn't you?"

"That stupid llama—the rock caught in its foot was a gold nugget. I kept going back, even GPS'd it, until I'd narrowed down the area where it was buried."

"And then you needed to buy time for Davenport and his men to find the gold. Were you always planning to kill them?"

Judith answered with a vague shrug. "They were always planning to kill me. Seriously? All that gold, who wouldn't? That's why I had their gear bugged. Even the ground-penetrating radar uploaded to a server I controlled—I knew they'd found the gold before they did. All I had to do was grab it, wait until things calmed down, and I'd be free of this godforsaken place forever. Until you came along."

"I still don't understand why you needed to get Bill out of the way. Your guys hadn't found the gold yet, they hadn't even started looking with the GPR. So Bill couldn't have seen anything. But you said he was close—"

Judith smiled. Not the grimace of someone who's been caught and was now regretting their actions, more like the grin of the Cheshire cat who had rained down chaos and was about to vanish without consequence. "You do realize that none of this girl talk matters? I could decide to let you live, and you still couldn't touch me. You can never prove anything, not even that I've said what I said. Even if you could, you can't arrest me. I'm sheriff now, so the only authority to arrest me would be the state police or the FBI. But...whoops...murder isn't a federal crime, is it? So not the FBI. And like I said, there's no proof of anything, so no state police either."

She nodded graciously at Lucy as if inviting her to tea. "Do go on. You were going to tell me where, hypothetically, if I did commit any of these hypothetically horrendous crimes, where I went wrong and how you figured out it was—hypothetically—me."

Judith was right. Lucy had no concrete proof, only vague suspicions—with time, she could establish a pattern, but it would be totally circumstantial, not enough to bring charges against Judith. The woman was too damn smart;

had covered her tracks too well. It was sheer dumb luck Bill had stumbled onto her crimes, and even he'd had had no inkling—at least not that Lucy could tell—that Judith was the perpetrator.

Or had he? That text sent to Judith. The one sent while they were in the plane. That couldn't have come from Bill, not if Judith killed him. Unless...

"You're wrong," Lucy said. "I can prove that you killed Bill."

"Oh, you think so? That's funny, since you're my alibi."

"I have a friend who's really, really good with electronics. Computers, phones, you name it. He can trace that final message from Bill to the app that sent it. The app you used to make it look like the text had come from Bill's phone and was sent before he was killed. But what really happened was you wrote the text and had it on a time delay, so it'd come when you had witnesses and could establish an alibi. If Bill died right after sending that text, there was no way you could have killed him. So once we found Bill's body, you were planning to fake the autopsy results, the body temperature, rigor mortis, time of death, so it all pointed to him dying after the text, not the day before. After all, you're the coroner, so who's going to argue? Especially when you're the one person with an airtight alibi since you were in the air with witnesses. But all it takes is one guy good with electronics, and then someone else will come in and re-do Bill's autopsy and find the truth. And then—"

Judith's laughter stopped Lucy cold. "You're making this way too complicated. Far easier to simply steal his phone and have someone send the text for me. Enough talk. Tabby's getting restless."

She hoisted the cattle prod in one hand, keeping the pistol in the other, and moved forward. No amount of talking was going to get her out of here, Lucy realized. She had to take control of the situation. And the only way to do that was to get close enough to tackle Judith.

Rush her? Or provoke her? Judith obviously enjoyed her games; liked to play with her victims. If she'd wanted to shoot Lucy, she would have done it already. At least Lucy hoped so—her life depended on it.

"You know what," Lucy continued. "I don't think you killed Bill after all. You're not smart enough to keep everyone guessing. There's no way you could have covered your tracks that well. I think you're the hired help. Davenport was right—there's someone else behind this. The real mastermind." She was pulling out every cliché from every bad thriller movie she could think of.

Judith's posture grew rigid, her shoulders hunching and face blazing with anger. She raised the pistol as if ready to pull the trigger, but her finger never went close. Instead Judith continued her march forward, holding the cattle prod like a lance. Lucy planted her feet, getting ready.

"Bottom line," Lucy served her *coup d'état*, "you don't have the brains. You're too damn stupid—"

Judith's shriek of anger cut past Lucy's next words, and the veterinarian stormed towards Lucy. Lucy waited for her to come within reach and braced herself against the railing as she lunged for the pistol—it could kill her, while the cattle prod would just hurt like hell. Judith triggered the cattle prod and electricity arched out, but Lucy whirled in time and it hit the steel railing, releasing a blaze of sparks that temporarily blinded Lucy. Then it died.

Before Lucy could recover and reach for Judith's pistol, Judith spun the metal cattle prod around, swinging it like a bat at Lucy's head.

Lucy twisted and raised her arm to soften the blow and protect her skull, grabbing at Judith's gun hand with the other. Judith heaved her weight against Lucy, toppling them both over the railing. And into the tiger pit.

Chapter 31

JUDITH BORE THE BRUNT OF THE FALL, landing on Tabby's favorite boulder, while Lucy ducked and rolled free, ending up in a clump of bushes. The tiger sprang out of the way of Judith's flailing arms and legs, seeming as stunned as the two women.

It growled, and Judith tried to hit it with the cattle prod. No electricity sparked, rendering it less than useless and more of an irritant to the large cat now baring its fangs. Judith raised her pistol and aimed between the cat's eyes.

"No!" Lucy shouted, lunging to put herself between Judith and the cat.

"You think I won't shoot you, too? Back

off before he attacks us both." Judith scrambled to her feet, balancing on the boulder. Lucy could feel the tiger's breath hot against her back. The cat was tensed up, panting and making a low rumbling noise deep in its throat.

Judith, now owning the higher ground, took aim at Tabby once again. Lucy pulled her walking stick free, whipped it out to its full length, and swung, taking Judith's legs out from under her. The gun went off, and the bullet hit the glass wall of the enclosure, the noise echoing through the cavernous space.

Lucy struck again, hitting Judith's wrist, and Judith dropped the pistol. Lucy dove for it just as a rush of air hit her from behind, followed by a sense of wonder as the tiger sprang. It flew over Lucy and pounced on Judith, swiping at her and sending her flying off the boulder.

Lucy found the gun in the bushes and grabbed it. But Judith was no longer a threat. She lay gasping for air, her clothes slashed, blood seeping through them. The wounds didn't appear deep, but they were enough to keep her down. Lucy backed away, her eyes on the tiger. Would it go after Judith again now that it had drawn first blood?

But Tabby seemed more interested in reclaiming his spot on the boulder, staring at the humans but not moving.

"Thank you," Lucy said in a soft voice. The cat nodded then began to lick his paws, still eyeing the two women warily.

She spotted a maintenance door behind Judith, on the other side of the enclosure from the tiger. Not taking her eyes off the cat, she backed up to it, dragging Judith, who was whimpering incoherently, with her. But before she opened the door, she stopped and looked down on the older woman.

"Tell me where Bill is or I'll leave you here for Tabby to play with."

The tiger made another one of those deep rumbles... if Lucy didn't know better, she'd think he understood her and was chuckling.

Judith blanched, pressing her hands against the deepest of her wounds. Blood seeped through her fingers. She'd be scarred for the rest of her life, lucky the cat hadn't targeted her face or neck. But after what she'd done, Lucy simply couldn't find it in her to care.

How many people had this woman killed? For nothing more than to feed her own ego. Lucy opened the door, edged through it to safety, and started to close it. "Last chance."

"Blanco Canyon. He's at Blanco Canyon."

"What happened?"

"I followed him out from Gus's place. He told me he was going to re-open my husband's death investigation. The fool thought I'd be excited, that I'd want to know the truth. Or maybe he was testing me, to see how I'd react. Either way, I couldn't let him dig into Max's death. Plus I knew he was suspicious about Davenport's men. He didn't buy that they were just geologists on a fishing trip. I'd heard Gus tell him about a good place to find huckleberries, a meadow above Blanco Canyon. When Bill turned up the road headed there, I followed him. It's a dead spot for everything—cell, satellite phones, GPS. Seemed perfect. I hit him with the cattle prod and pushed him over the cliff. That's where you'll find his body. Blanco Canyon."

Tabby yawned and shifted his position on the boulder, eyeing Judith like she was a midnight snack.

"I told you everything," Judith insisted. "Now get me the hell away from that damn cat!"

THE STATE POLICE RESCUE HELICOPTER found Bill exactly where Lucy had told them he was. She only wished she could have gone herself, but instead, once she'd turned Judith over to her own deputies along with the staties, Harriet drove Lucy over to Deena's to wait for word from the rescue team.

Finally the radio crackled. "Rescue three for Magruder two, do you copy?"

Deena's hand was trembling so hard that Lucy reached past her for the handset. "Magruder two, copy. You have Mrs. Beachey here." She wanted them to know that Deena was there in case they were sending bad news.

Thankfully, good news always came faster than bad. “We found him. He’s hurt but alive. We’ve got him in the helo and are flying direct to Harborview Trauma Center. He says to tell Deena not to worry.”

Deena’s mom and sister clapped their hands while Deena slumped against Lucy, speechless.

“Tell Bill she’s gonna kill him for making her worry,” Lucy said, knowing that would make Bill smile. “And that she’ll meet him in Seattle.”

“Ten-four. Rescue three out.”

Chapter 32

THANKS TO ONE OF THE charter pilots ferrying them, Lucy and Deena arrived at the trauma center only a few hours after Bill. He was in surgery most of the night, but in the meantime, Nick had his ankle casted and was discharged, while Gleason was admitted. Thankfully, they were informed, he'd be fine.

The sun was up before the surgeon finally came to the waiting room where Nick and Lucy were sitting with Deena. "Your husband was quite lucky. In a way, the combination of his blood loss, mild hypothermia, and dehydration saved his life—it kept his blood pressure low enough that the bleeding and swelling from his skull fracture weren't immediately life-threatening. But it was a good thing we found him when we did."

Deena squeezed Lucy's hand at that. "So he'll be all right?"

"He should make a full recovery," the surgeon assured her. "Though it'll take a while. In addition to the head trauma, he suffered a subcapsular splenic hematoma that we'll be monitoring, but I think he'll be able to keep his spleen. Broken zygoma, broken humerus, bilateral rib fractures—but luckily no pneumothorax. Right hip displacement, which we surgically reduced while we repaired his lacerated saphenous vein. And we had to do an open reduction of his tib-fib fracture on the left, but it looks like there's no permanent nerve damage or vascular compromise." The surgeon paused, as if waiting for applause. "You'll be able to see him soon. He's just waking up from the anesthesia."

Then he left. Deena appeared stunned. Lucy jumped in to translate—she'd been through the drill enough times with victims, medical reports, and, unfortunately, her own injuries. "There's a bit of bleeding around his spleen that they're watching. A broken cheekbone and a broken arm. No collapsed lung, but a few cracked ribs—"

"So don't make him laugh," Nick added, his arm wrapped around his own bruised ribs.

"They fixed his hip, and he had a broken leg as well—but instead of a cast, he'll have pins and screws and braces on both the inside and outside of his leg, just to help it mend faster."

Nick winced at that and reached for Lucy's hand. She was sure he was remembering her own Erector Set nightmare of hardware from January.

Later that afternoon, Deena escorted Nick and Lucy in to see Bill. His head was swathed in bandages, both eyes were blackened and almost swelled shut, IVs were running in one arm while the other was in a cast and bound to his chest, one leg was bristling with hardware, and monitor wires were attached to everything from head to toe.

But he was alive, if not quite awake. They sat for a while with Deena while Bill dozed, occasionally waking enough for her to give him a sip of water.

"What about the animals in Judith's zoo?" Deena asked.

"I asked Gleason about them," Lucy answered. "He says he knows a rich guy with a spread over in Big Sky who has a licensed wildlife sanctuary." She'd been glad to learn that Tabby's attack wasn't going to be held against the tiger. After all, if anything, he'd shown considerable restraint. More than Lucy had—threatening a wounded woman. She cringed with shame at the thought of it, but then looked at Bill's fingers wrapped around Deena's and just couldn't find it in her to be remorseful. Which maybe she should be even more ashamed of, she wasn't sure.

"Funny," Lucy continued, "but in a way Bill came out the winner. I know that sounds weird, but to the end, all Judith kept asking, what drove her to keep going when she could have walked away scot free, wasn't the gold. Instead, she was obsessed with knowing where she'd gone wrong. She just couldn't believe Bill was smarter than her."

Deena smiled. "Bill is tons smarter than most people gave him credit for. He pays attention; that's his secret weapon."

Nick rocked against his crutches, redistributing his weight away from his injured leg. "I know why Bill suspected that Max didn't die of an accidental snakebite."

Lucy and Deena turned to him. "You do? What was it?"

"The snakes," came a hoarse whisper from the bed. Bill's eyes fluttered as open as they could given the swelling. "I asked her. About the snakes."

"They were counterfeit," Nick said.

"What do you mean?"

"I think I've put together the pieces Bill hadn't had a chance to gather. Max Keenan died from a coral snake bite, right? Judith didn't fake his autopsy—in fact, since she was next of kin, she asked the Idaho County coroner to perform his death investigation."

"Right," Lucy said. "He died from coral snake envenomation. But there was a coral snake there—Max's DNA was recovered from it and its cage. And Judith's alibi was rock solid. So how could that be counterfeit?"

"She switched the snake," Nick answered. "All the time Max was displaying those snakes, they weren't the real thing—they were lookalikes. Harriet gave me the original shipping invoices, and I found old videos and photos from tourists—it was tough because the thick glass on the snake habitats was designed to warp any efforts to get a close look or take clear photos, but if you look at enough of the pictures—or if, like Bill, you get real photos of the dead animals that were included in Max's autopsy report, you can see. The so-called copperhead was actually a corn snake, the water moccasin was a regular brown water snake, the black mamba was a racer snake, and so on. Except the coral snake. That was real—at least the one that killed Max was. But the original shipping information was for *lampropeltis triangulum annulata*."

"In English?" Lucy asked, but she couldn't hide her smile. Nick was so damned cute when he geeked out.

"Mexican milk snake."

"Because he'd stocked the exhibit with harmless lookalikes, Max thought the snakes couldn't hurt him? So he wasn't worried when one bit him?" Deena asked.

"Maybe he didn't know," Bill said, his voice growing stronger.

"Right," Nick said. "Real coral snakes have such sharp fangs that their bite can be painless. However it happened, Judith switched the snakes, created an alibi for when Max was due to clean the cages, and bang, the perfect crime."

"Until Bill came along and started asking questions," Deena said proudly.

"Until Bill came along," Nick repeated. "The only lawman in four decades smart enough to suspect Judith of murder."

Lucy wrapped her arm around Nick and leaned into him. "Pretty clever, Dr. Callahan. I knew there was a reason I married you."

"Here I thought it was for my looks." He glanced at the clock. "We have to go, or we're going to be late." He grabbed his crutches and started for the door.

Bill frowned. "Go where?"

Lucy rolled her eyes. "Nick decided I needed a second opinion about my leg. So he called in a favor."

She went to Bill and bent over to plant a kiss on a small patch of his forehead that didn't appear too badly bruised. "Glad to have you back with us."

"Glad to be here." He reached for her arm, his IV tubing clacking against the bed rail. "Lucy, thanks."

"You'd do the same for me. Besides, I wasn't alone."

"Good luck," Deena called out, as Lucy joined Nick out in the hall.

They walked across the medical center to the outpatient complex. "You know," he said as he hopped along beside her with his crutches, "your ankle splint and walking stick saved the day."

"Along with Megan's paracord bracelet. She's never going to let me live that down, asking her to make me another one." They reached the clinic door, and she turned to him. “Wait. Are you saying you’re okay either way? If I keep my leg, even if I never get better than I am now?”

He nestled his crutches against his body and pulled her close. “I’m happy with whatever you decide. Just saying, you’re pretty damn perfect already. If anyone cares about my opinion.”

She pulled the door open and held it for him. “Let’s just see what Gleason’s mom has to say. Then we can decide.”

Chapter 33

Lucy held Nick's hand as they sat in Gleason's mother's office. Unlike the other surgeons Lucy had dealt with, Dr. Annette Gleason believed in allowing her patients to get dressed and join her in her office for treatment discussions rather than having them wait in sterile and intimidating exam rooms. She also didn't crowd her office walls with large gilt-framed diplomas. Instead, her walls held artwork and photographs from her medical missions to Malawi, the Congo, Pakistan, Haiti, and Syria.

She knocked on her own office door before entering. Dr. Gleason was older than Lucy's other surgeons, in her mid to late fifties, with dark hair streaked with gray. She was fit and trim—every orthopedic surgeon Lucy had met had that in common—but she moved with the grace of a ballet dancer rather than the stride of an athlete.

"Do you guys need anything? Coffee? Juice? We don't offer pop because the sugar and carbonation are deadly to bone health."

Lucy squeezed Nick's hand, too nervous to answer. "No thanks, we're good," he said. "Thanks for seeing us so quickly."

"Least I could do after you saved my son's life." She beamed at a photo of Gleason hanging behind her desk. He was in his official Forest Service uniform, complete with Smokey the Bear hat tilted at a rakish angle. "I'm not sure I'll ever find a way to fully repay you for that."

Dr. Gleason took the empty seat beside them. Another surprise—Lucy had expected her to sit down behind the desk. The doctor placed her tablet in front of them and inclined it so they could all see it. She brushed her finger, and an X-ray of Lucy's ankle appeared. She'd recognize that chaos of hardware anywhere.

"Bottom line," she said before Dr.

Gleason could start. "Does it need to come off?"

The surgeon took her time before answering. And in that pause, Lucy felt herself relaxing, breathing out her anxiety and inhaling a sense of...release. Nick was right. Relinquishing control, not constantly trying to outwit fate—it felt good. Not because Lucy didn't care what happened to her body, but because she knew she'd be fine—they'd be fine—either way.

Beyond the office door, a printer's rumble sounded almost like the growl of a snarling dog. Almost. Lucy banished the whiff of memory before it could take hold, and focused on the surgeon.

"Come off? Would da Vinci slice off the *Mona Lisa*'s smile? Your ankle is a masterpiece. Not just the surgical feat of engineering but also the work you've put in rehabilitating it." She zoomed out and up to higher on the leg where there were only bones. "Look at that bone density. Excellent."

"The other doctor said my bones were too old to heal properly, and that was why we needed to consider amputation."

Dr. Gleason made a tutting noise. "Sometimes it's easier to blame the patient than look for the real cause, especially in cases like yours where there's every expectation of failure, given the type of trauma and severe damage you sustained."

"So, you're saying she can keep the leg?" Nick leaned forward. "But what about the pain?"

"Tell me more about it. Given your nerve damage, I'd expect the electrical shocks and muscle fasciculations, early on. Are those staying the same, getting worse, or becoming less frequent?"

"Not as often and a little less severe."

"Definitely not startling her out of her sleep like they used to," Nick added.

"Is there a new pain, then? One interfering with proper function?"

"Yes. I just thought it was the same pain—they always blamed the nerve damage—evolving. But it's deeper, and almost constant even when I'm not using the leg. Worse with running and walking."

The surgeon nodded. She touched the screen again, this time zooming in to one area of bone pierced by screws and a plate. "Do you see here? The slight angle this screw is taking? Wait—you can see it better on this view. Here, where the screw is forced away from neutral by this band of tissue it's impinging on? It's rather subtle, but I think at high magnification you can see it."

Lucy tried to interpret the shades of gray on the screen. "Kind of. It looks like the screw wants to go in straight, but that tissue is blocking it. Is that my nerve?"

"Exactly right. As your nerves healed—and I suspect also as the bone healed after you fought the osteomyelitis, the infection in it—this screw began to pinch the outer sheaf of the nerve. That led to inflammation—"

"Which caused the pain," Nick finished for her, sounding triumphant. "That infection was why she had to stay in the hospital for so long and had several operations to clean out the damaged tissues."

Lucy didn't remember most of that time—it was all a haze of pain and fever dreams. She'd been sick enough that she'd been in the ICU the first few days, but she really hadn't known what was going on, not until she woke up days later to find Nick asleep in a chair beside her hospital bed, his head bowed over her chest as if listening for her heart beat, one hand entwined in hers.

He was the one who'd consented to the surgeries instead of the amputation the first doctors had wanted back then. Which was why Lucy tried never to let him see how much pain she was really in.

"The problem with bone infections is that even after the infection is gone, they can cause havoc with any hardware. And, to be honest, as long as you have the hardware an infection can return. So, we have two options."

"Amputation?" Nick asked.

"Yes. It would be below the knee—actually, we have quite a lot to work with as far as favorable tissue. Rehab would take some time, but quite frankly, other than the daily management of the stump and prosthesis, your function would be the same as what you have now or even improved. I have patients who run marathons after—in fact, their main complaint is that their non-prosthetic limb slows them down."

"What's the second option?" Lucy asked.

"We can replace the screw—and while we're in there, we'll also grab a sample and culture it to see if there's any new infection complicating things, but I doubt it. You'd also need to cut back on your rehab for a short period, just to avoid aggravating things, but you could still do normal activities as you felt like it. And that's the key here: not pushing yourself to heal faster but instead giving your body a break and letting it heal at its own pace."

Lucy grimaced. The concept went against every instinct, but she'd try. "So you think I can keep my leg?"

"Yes, I do." Dr. Gleason's smile was as reassuring as the scent of home-baked cookies. Something about this woman radiated not only confidence—Lucy had seen plenty of that from her other surgeons—but also comfort and serenity. For the first time in a long while, Lucy felt able to relax and place her trust in someone. She could keep her leg, keep her job, keep working on the rest of everything with Nick and Megan. It seemed all too simple—not the fight she was used to.

"And all you need me to do is take it easy?" Lucy asked.

Nick chuckled at that. "Doctor, you have no idea—"

"Oh, believe me, I think I do. But the bottom line here is that the choice is yours. Not mine."

Lucy glanced at Nick, who nodded as he intertwined his fingers in hers. "I want to keep it. It's a part of me. I know that might not make sense—"

"No, it makes perfect sense. Sometimes we just need a reminder that it's okay to stop fighting and take care of ourselves. Maybe this is that time for you."

Lucy blinked hard at the surgeon's words. Now she understood what Nick had been trying to tell her: that not fighting, not constantly struggling, was not the same as surrendering. She could still do what she did and take care of her family…and herself. She just couldn't do it all, not all the time. Not without losing a piece of herself.

"So, we'll take it one step at a time," Dr. Gleason said.

Lucy couldn't agree more.

"You were right," she whispered to Nick. He smiled back with only his eyes; his Buddha smile, she liked to call it. She squeezed his hand and never felt so lucky.

About CJ:

New York Times and *USA Today* bestselling author of over forty novels, former pediatric ER doctor CJ Lyons has lived the life she writes about in her cutting-edge Thrillers with Heart.

Two-time winner of the International Thriller Writers' coveted Thriller Award, CJ has been called a "master within the genre" (Pittsburgh Magazine) and her work has been praised as "breathtakingly fast-paced" and "riveting" (Publishers Weekly) with "characters with beating hearts and three dimensions" (Newsday).

Learn more about CJ's Thrillers with Heart at www.CJLyons.net

88560250R00210

Made in the USA
Middletown, DE
10 September 2018